Canaries:
Story of Forgiveness

D1522614

Canaries: Story of Forgiveness

Written by David Wilkes

XULON PRESS

Xulon Press
2301 Lucien Way #415
Maitland, FL 32751
407.339.4217
www.xulonpress.com

Paperback ISBN-13: 978-1-6628-3691-6
Ebook ISBN-13: 978-1-6628-3692-3

Contents

Chapter 1

De'Ninos Way !

t was late one Thursday evening in the autumn of 2008. Sylvester De Nino was taking a breather in his car, ready to leave from work. Sylvester worked as an architect drafter for his father named Dean who owned an architecture company called, "De Nino's Pillar" in East Haven, Connecticut. Sylvester then drove away and within a few minutes receives a phone call from his wife named Marie, home four months pregnant. Sylvester said, "Hello?" Marie answered, "Hey, where are ya? I thought you be home by now." Sylvester was only a few minutes from the house, making a right turn into the street where they live. Sylvester replied, "I'm about to pull into the driveway now; did you need something?" Marie thought on the comment, leaving the living room and walking into the kitchen, away from their two daughters. Monica, age fourteen, with Renee, age thirteen, were seated on the couch watching a sitcom.

1

They lived inside a five bedroom, two bathrooms, two-story home with one garage and a basement in the suburbs of East Haven, Connecticut.

Marie then sat at the kitchen table and answered, "No, were you backed up with work?" Sylvester arrived in the garage and got out saying, "Yeah, also earlier I was talking to Paul on the phone. I'm coming inside now." Paul Lagaipa was his friend throughout the years. Marie then hung up; Sylvester came inside the front door. Monica and Renee continued watching TV until the door shuts. Monica turned around and saw her father; she smiled and said, "Hey Pop !" Sylvester waved, answering, "Hey ! Hey !" Renee then saw her father, smiled, and continued to watch TV. Sylvester then went into the kitchen and saw Marie seated at the kitchen table. Marie said, "If you are hungry, your food is already in the refrigerator." Sylvester smiled and slowly answered, "I'm fine. I'm thinking about going into business with Paul." Marie, wondering what kind of business with her arms crossed, asked, "OH? . ... What kind of business?" Marie then looked at the clock on the wall and saw it was 8:55 pm. Marie looked to the living room, seated close, yelled, "HEY, GIRLS, IT'S GETTING LATE ! . ...TIME FOR BED !" Renee then got upset and looked at Monica, saying, "Let's go, Chi Chi ! I don't think it's late." The girls then headed upstairs to their rooms. Sylvester took a set at the kitchen table to better explain himself. Sylvester responded, "Art gallery ! Trying it out, Marie; you never know. In the future, the kids could run it; Paul's kid also." Marie then got up, putting a dirty dish from the table into the sink. Marie looked at Sylvester and began to worry, saying, "Sylvester, I don't know. There is something not right with Paul. How's things with your father's company?" Sylvester answered, "Good. He's still sick though. He told me he has a buyer."

Marie, curious about the remark, replied, "I don't understand? You said things were good; what buyer?" Sylvester got up and walked over to Marie to better explain answers, "My father and I had a meeting with a buyer named Omar Lugo. They know each other. Omar wants to buy the company to improve it. Omar already owns an architecture company named, Sledge in Hamden. He comes from a family of money is what I hear." Marie, using a little sarcasm, replied, "Ya don't say. So, is your father selling or . … ?" Sylvester began to scratch his bald head and answered, "We don't know yet. But are you ready for this?" Marie, with a puzzled look, asked, "Ready for what?" Sylvester smiled, then continued to say, "Omar wants to buy us out for ten million dollars !" Marie, at a loss for words, then took a second touching her heart and responded, "OH MY GOD ! OH MY GOD ! Sylvester !" Sylvester then answered back in a funny manner, "My God too ! It's my father's decision !" Marie, still concerned about the comment earlier, stared at Sylvester, and said, "If you're gonna do business with Paul, be careful; I don't trust him." Sylvester, feeling confident, looked into her eyes and said, "Everything will be all right !" They both kissed, then went upstairs to bed for the evening.

The next morning, outside a waste management building in downtown New Haven, run by Sylvester's friend named Bird Lombardi, Paul was talking with Bird about the idea partnership with Sylvester at the front entrance. Paul had a goatee with dark, short, gelled hair and was dressed casually. Bird was short and solid with short, dark hair. Bird, being impatient, replied, "De Nino, right? What did he say?" Paul smiled and answered, "He said yes. If he's like his father, together we will make money." Bird, not being moved, replied, "Paul ! . ... You ain't no artist ! . ... I understand you two being friends and all. But .... Being business partners is a bad idea." Bird, with a serious look, continued to say, "Paul, I know you !" Paul got upset about the comment and replied back, "What do you mean you know me? I know I did five years in jail for a robbery and ... " Paul, being heated, then lifts his hands up, saying, "Why do I even with you, Bird? Don't you have a business to run !" Paul reached for his keys in his pocket, walking away frustrated. Bird smirked at Paul going to his car. Bird yelled, "Your character ain't right for business ! Sylvester had gotten soft with ya ! It won't work ! Go home to your wife and son, Paul !" Paul then frowned and out of anger yelled, "WELL, YOU AND SYLVESTER CAN'T BE RIGHT FOR FRIENDSHIP THEN ! . ... YOU BOTH HAD THE SAME WOMAN, SO DON'T START WITH ME BIRD ! . ... MARIE IS NO LONGER GIOVE,

BUT DE NINO AND HAPPY, BRO !" Bird then got upset, looked around, and, seeing no employees, speedily replied," You know what you can do for me, Paul?" Paul then immediately drove away, ignoring Bird. Bird yelled out, "YEAH, WELL DON'T DO ME ANY FAVORS !" Bird turned around, then walked inside the building with the thought of calling Sylvester regarding the matter.

Sylvester, that same morning, was in the bathroom, dressed casually for work with the door opened. Sylvester checked himself before leaving the bathroom and out loud said, "It's only business, nothing serious." Marie was sitting on their bed facing the bathroom, dressed ready to run errands. Marie smiled at Sylvester and said, "You look fine, hun !" Sylvester then came out the bathroom and looked at her stomach, asking, "How are you feel? How's our son?" Marie got up and answered, "I'm fine. The girls normally help me around the house, you know. They're excited to have a brother." Sylvester's phone around the bedroom dresser started to vibrate. Marie then got up and got his phone answered, "Hello?" Marie then received shocking news that touched her heart. Marie yelled, "OH MY GOD ! . ... IT'S YOUR FATHER ! DEAN COLLAPSED !" Marie then asked which hospital. Sylvester stood next to her, waiting for the information, worried. Marie told Sylvester the New Haven hospital and that Lewis was on the phone. Marie then yelled out of being anxious, "WE'LL BE RIGHT THERE !"

Sylvester, with Marie, left quickly to the New Haven hospital. They rushed inside and checked in. The nurse asked, "Who are you looking for?" Sylvester panicking answered, "Dean De Nino ! He is my father. What room is he in?" The nurse had shown them the emergency room but couldn't let them in. Standing outside the room was a short and lean manager from De Nino's Pillar named Lewis, greeting them. Lewis watching the nurse leave said, "I'm glad you got my call. They're doing the best they can with this heart attack situation." Sylvester then began pacing back and forth, worried. Marie stood with Lewis waiting near the door. Sylvester, being curious, asked, "What happened in detail?" Lewis then walked over to Sylvester and answered, "Dean and I were in his office. He said he wasn't feeling well. He then collapses walking to his desk. Immediately I called for an ambulance ! Dean has been sick for some time now." Lewis looked at his watch and replied, "I'll check on your father tomorrow." Lewis, worried not knowing what else to say, left. Marie then walked over and comfort Sylvester with a hug, and looking into his eyes says, "They're helping your father as best as they can; he will get better." That same nurse came back around the corner to check on everyone. She waved them over, saying, "Come to the waiting room." They then followed the nurse and got settled in the waiting room, with Sylvester still worried for his father. After a few hours of waiting around, it then became 2:45 pm. A nurse came over and said, "We need to keep your father for a while. This is what I was told to tell you guys." Sylvester and Marie got up and left the hospital troubled.

Monica, around that time, invited a fifteen-year-old guy she liked from school named Jason over to the house. Renee knew about Jason; she was downstairs seated on the floor, watching a thriller movie. Monica and Jason were kissing in her room. Jason stopped and got nervous in regards to getting caught. Jason asked," Monica, will your parents be home soon?" Monica laughed at the comment and said, "No. Are you scared?" Monica then checked her window and didn't see her father's car. Jason asked," Are they here?" Monica turned around and answered," No, now are you gonna kiss me or what?" Jason smiled, walking over to her, and they started making out again. Jason then stopped again and said, "I never kissed a girl before." Monica got excited and replied, "Really?" Renee, at that time, gets up from the living room floor. She went into the kitchen for popcorn and heard her parents pulling up in the garage. Renee at once took off and ran upstairs knocking on Monica's door. Renee yelled, "CHI CHI ! CHI CHI !"

Jason and Monica heard the knocks and stop talking. Jason, being unfamiliar with the name, questioned Monica, "Who is Chi Chi?" Monica then ran to the door, nervous and opened it quickly. She panicked, looking at Renee and asked, "What is it?" Renee stared worried that they would get caught. She looked downstairs, then back at Monica, saying, "They are here ! What are you gonna do?" They then heard the front door opened. Marie with Sylvester were conversating about his father. Marie then looked around the living room with the TV on pondering where the girls were. She, placing her purse on the couch, yelled, "RENEE ! .... MONICA ! ... GIRLS, WHERE ARE YOU?" Sylvester got her attention, pointing upstairs, hearing the girls talk. Renee quickly ran downstairs and met Sylvester at the bottom steps into the living room. Marie then sat on the couch, not seeing Monica, and asked, "Where's your sister? What's she doing?"Renee, ignoring the question, asked, "Did you need help making dinner tonight?" Marie answered," You know what, I do. I have so many things on my mind right now. Did you have lunch yet?" Renee answered, "No." Marie then frowned and said, "Renee, hun? There is food in the refrigerator."The movie then came to a killing scene. Marie saw and didn't like it yelled, "RENEE, COULD YA TURN THE CHANNEL TO SOMETHING ELSE? .... SOMETHING UPLIFTING !" Renee then turned the channel, hoping Monica didn't get caught.

Jason then slowly opened her door and looked down the hallway. Jason heard someone coming upstairs. He saw no one, then quickly closed the door back and left. Jason then headed to the bathroom down the hall with a mind to open the window to escape. Sylvester then made it upstairs and looked down the hall and caught Jason. Sylvester, caught off guard, yelled, "HEY, COME HERE !" Jason then turned around in shock and with his head down, came to Sylvester, feeling shameful. Sylvester, not knowing what was going on, replied, "Who are you and where is Monica?" Jason answered, "I'm her friend Jason from school; she's in her room." Monica heard everything and began fixing herself up. Monica than heard a knock at her door. She took a breather, not ready for questions, and opened. Monica saw Jason standing with his head down feeling discomfort; Sylvester behind him with a disappointed stare at her. Renee, around that time, was watching TV and left the living room. She went into the kitchen with her mother to help start dinner. Marie about to question her, she saw and quickly replied, "Chi Chi is doing her hair, Mom." Marie nodded, then went into the deep refrigerator for fish.

Sylvester, with a no-nonsense view, asked, "Who is he and how old?" Monica, with an attitude, rolled her eyes and answers, "Jason, he is my boyfriend. And he is fifteen." Jason, still looking down and avoiding eye contact, replied, "I'm sorry, sir !" Sylvester looked at them in a calm manner and, balling his fists, asked, "If your mother and I weren't here, what would have happened?" Monica, avoided looking at her father with her arms crossed and head down, answered, "Nothing !" Sylvester then put his arms to his hips, saying, "Jason, you follow me. For the record I forgive you two; don't let this happen again ! Your mother will not know about this ! And I will talk to Renee if she's involved too." Monica then walked to her father and hugged him.

Sylvester received the hug, had calm down. Monica said, "Sorry Dad."

Sylvester, with Jason, then went downstairs, passing the living room. Marie and Renee were both busy fixing dinner. Marie heard the door opened and closed, asked, "Who was that?" Renee swiftly answers, "Dad or Chi Chi, I don't know. Monica, at the time, was taking another breather around the mirror, holding her heart with the thought being this can't happen again. Monica then went downstairs to give her mother a hand in the kitchen. Monica then winked at Renee, reaching in the cabinet for pepper to season. Sylvester and Jason stood near the front door. Jason knew he needed to say something replied, "Hey, Mr. De Nino? With your permission, can I see your daughter?" Sylvester smirked at the remark, looking to the sky replied, "Monica is my daughter. I want what's best for her. Jason, my question to you is are you what's best for her?" Sylvester waited for Jason's answer, with his hands in his pockets. Jason, looking unsure, answered, "I think I am, Mr. De Nino." Sylvester smiled and placed his hand on Jason's shoulder and, in a mild tone of voice, responded, "Hey, maybe someday you'll surprise me. Right? Stay away from her. Now …. Have a good day, Jason." Jason then walked away with his head down. Sylvester watched him leave, then went back inside the house.

Later in the afternoon, the De Nino's were having dinner. The girls had made fried fish and spaghetti with sauce, and they all enjoyed it. Marie looking at the girls then asked, "So, how was your day, girls?" Monica made eye contact with Renee, not knowing what to say. Renee answered, "I didn't really do much today; nothing was on TV...Say, Mom? Have you thought of a name for our brother yet?" Monica got excited about the remark and, in a sarcastic manner, replied, "Yeah ! Nothing crazy I hope !" Marie looked at Sylvester with a worried look answers, "Your father and I came from the hospital. Your Grandpa had a heart attack."Sylvester, thinking of his father, gazed at them and replied, "We believe he will pull through; we haven't decided on a name yet." Marie immediately comforted Sylvester by touching his hand. Sylvester looked at her, feeling confident about the situation. Monica and Renee began to worry about their grandfather. Marie, feeling uplifted, saw the girls' reactions and said, "Girls ! Your father is gonna open an art gallery with his friend, Paul. Isn't that wonderful?" Monica and Renee were surprised, got excited, and encouraged their father. Marie smiled at the encouragement and said, "John 15:7 is what I told your father. If the Lord's Word abides in you, ask and it shall be done." Sylvester smiled at everyone, then began to kiss Marie. Sylvester, with sarcasm, replied, "My father's healing is what I want done. I'm just now hearing this, Marie !" The girls then began to laugh at the remark. Within an hour, they all went to their rooms ready for bed, excited about the art gallery.

Two days later, in the morning, at the De Nino's residence, Sylvester's phone had vibrated on the bed dresser. Sylvester got up and reached for his phone. Seeing it was Lewis's number, answered it and said, "Lewis, what's up?" Lewis, in a merry manner, replied, "Hey Sylvester! Your father wants to see you. He keeps asking about you. I know it's almost eight in the morning. You're coming down, right?" Sylvester, bare chested and wearing pajama pants, then got up and opened his closet door, responding, "Tell him I'm on my way!" Sylvester then hung up looking at pants while Marie woke up. Sylvester then turned around and looked at Marie lying in bed, saying, "I'm going to see my father; I'll be back." Marie gazed at Sylvester and replied, "Honey, shower first and send him our love." Sylvester answered," Good point." Sylvester then went into the bathroom to shower.

When Sylvester arrived at the hospital after checking in, he met with Lewis again standing outside Dean's room. Lewis then greeted Sylvester, opened and closed the door for him, saying, "I'll wait out here." Sylvester then saw his father relaxing on his bed, looking well. Dean waved him to come over. Sylvester came and kissed him on the cheek, asking, "How are you feeling? Are you ready to come back home?" Dean laughed at the comment and answers, "I am; the food here is terrible. How's the family?" Sylvester, in concern for his father, repeated the question again, "How are you feeling?" Dean then frowned at his son and answered, "Never mind how I feel!" Sylvester said, "Marie is now four months pregnant; the girls are fine. Dean then smiled at Sylvester. Dean then faced the window to the right. Dean, in thought of the future, replied, "Listen, son ! If anything happens to me." Sylvester then waved his hands in disapproval, not wanting to hear it.

Dean stared at Sylvester with a demanding voice, saying, "Your gonna hear me anyways, Sylvester ! Now, come closer and listen to me." Sylvester came closer, then his father continued to say, "This is the second time this has happened to me, you know this !" Sylvester then took two steps back and answered, "Go on !" Dean calmed down, watching his son walk slowly says, "I'm going to sell the company to Omar. ... ... I am giving you the ten million that was offered; my family will not see poverty. I wanted you to continue running the company. I know it's not in you to do so . .... I am taken care of financially; don't worry about me."

Sylvester, at a loss for words, answered, "Ten million? You had this company since the late seventies." Dean laughed at the remark and said, "What I am doing is Proverbs 13:22. You heard it growing up: 'A good man leaves an inheritance to his children's children.'" Sylvester, still worried about his father's health, replied, "So, when are you coming home?" Sylvester's phone in his jacket started to vibrate. He reached into the pocket and saw it was Marie. Dean responded, "I should know today if I can go home or not. Can you turn the TV on? My lawyer has looked over the contract and I signed before this had happened." Sylvester, amazed at the remark, turned the TV on and said, "Hey !" Marie answers, "Hey, listen ! Bird came looking for you. He gave cannoli's with chocolate chips in them for us and your father. Alright, Bye babe." Marie then hung up. Sylvester looked back at his father and laughed. Dean said, "Why are you laughing at me? What's funny?" Sylvester, knowing his father loved cannoli's with chocolate chips in them, answered, "Love those cannoli's !" They both laughed at the comment.

Sylvester then received a phone call from Bird so he picked up and said," Bird, I've been meaning to call you. What's up?" Bird answered," So, Paul spoken to me about a partnership between you both. An art gallery?" Sylvester began to walk away from his father, waving to him goodbye. Dean saw and waved back, watching TV. Sylvester, leaving the room, then stood in the hallway, not seeing Lewis, and said," I believe people can change, Bird. What are you asking me?" Bird replied, "Let me be there for you as a friend, De Nino, is what I am asking." Sylvester then checked his watch and said," Alright, let's have a meeting today at the café on Second Avenue. You meet me now and you call Paul !" Bird answered," I'm on my way." Sylvester then hung up and left the hospital for the meeting.

Around that time, Paul and his short, slim wife with long, dark hair named Stephanie were arguing about his drinking habit in the kitchen of their home. Their teenage son named,

Carmin was in bed and heard everything. Upset, he couldn't sleep pulling the covers over his head. Stephanie replied, "Our son needs you ! This has to stopped; it needs to stop ! "Paul ignored the remark and looked away. She raises her voice louder to get his attention. Paul then got angry and said, "Will you shut up? Poor kid can't even sleep in his room because of you ! Steph, our son can hear you !" Stephanie immediately calmed down and lowered her voice. She then got in his face, saying, "You're an alcoholic. It's killing our family; look at you !" She took a breather, then continues on to say, "If not for me, then do it for your son ! This is killing our family, think about it." Stephanie began to shed tears, knowing he won't change. Paul avoided eye contact, looking down. Paul then changed the subject and answered, "Sylvester and I are gonna make money together. We will be debt-free from all our debts. We are gone to open up an art gallery. Stephanie.. Believe in me, believe in us !" Stephanie then shook her head, with tears streaming down her cheeks, feeling under minded and confuse. Stephanie said, "I don't understand you !" She then walked away, feeling empty inside to their room. She slammed the door shut, and leaned against the wall crying.

Paul stared at their door feeling undermined, then received a call. Paul checked his phone and saw it was Sylvester's number. Paul said, "Hello?" Paul began to hear Bird's voice answer, "Listen !" Paul immediately interrupted, asking, "Bird, why are you talking to me? Isn't this Sylvester's number?" Bird laughed at the remark, answering, "Sylvester and I are friends also, whether you like it or not. Sylvester told me to call you for a meeting right now at the café on Second Avenue. Can you make it?" Paul began to get a little nervous on the mention so he asked, "The café on second Avenue, just the three of us? Why?" Bird responded, "One. I am godfather to his children. And two, Sylvester wants to go over a few things with you. So, you're coming?" Paul, looking at his watch, said, "I'll be there. Question, why didn't Sylvester call me?" Bird then laughed out loud and answered, "Because I intervened. You have a problem with that?" Paul, feeling a situation might occur, with confidence replied, "See you then."

Paul then hung up, wondering what was going on. Bird smiled sitting across Sylvester, giving his phone back at the café. Sylvester watched customers come and go while drinking a small coffee, black with two sugars. Bird asked, "Did your father get the cannoli's?" Sylvester chuckled, then answered, "Tomorrow he will." They laughed at the remark as a waiter came over to see if they needed anything else.

Paul showed up an hour later at the café on Second Avenue. Paul was dressed casual with a short, black leather coat. Paul was chewing gum, smelling like alcohol but ready for the meeting. The waiter at the front desk glanced at Paul and asked, "Table for one, sir?" Paul gazed at the people there. Paul then spotted Bird with Sylvester and answers,

"I'm with the bald and healthy gentlemen, the last table to the left." Paul being curious asked, "How long have those two been here?" The waiter, giving his full attention, answered, "A little over an hour." Bird saw Paul then tap Sylvester on the shoulder to get his attention. Sylvester then saw Paul and checked his watch as he came over. Paul then took a seat at their table and, after being stared at, said, "This was short notice so I can't be late, you know. So, what's up?" Bird and Sylvester then looked at each other in concern for the future partnership with Paul. Bird then went ahead in a no-nonsense manner, saying, "Sylvester, I got to say this ! ….Paul, I don't think you're good for any partnership of any business. You have a habit of being late and you are an alcoholic. ….Consider this an intervention from me, Paul !

Sylvester then calmed Bird down by raising his hand. Bird got up, feeling disturbed, and started walking out of the café. Paul then spit the gum out of his mouth and, with sarcasm, said, "Did you have to bring him? I am trying, Sylvester; believe me I am." Sylvester stared at Paul, taking a breather, and answers, "Paul, we shouldn't do business. Bird is making perfect sense . …I have a son on the way. Why you ? You know . …" Paul then interrupted, feeling confused, making a sarcastic, loud comment, "IS THAT WHY BIRD'S THE GODFATHER TO YOUR SON? ….WHY ARE YOU LISTENING TO HIM? …. THIS IS BETWEEN ME AND YOU, DE NINO! … ARE YOU TWO GOING INTO BUSINESS?" Paul's voice had gotten so loud that the manager came over and questioned whether everything was all right. Paul, being upset, replied, "Nobody called you over ! You need to turn around and mind your business !" Sylvester stopped Paul by raising his hand. He then apologized to the manager for Paul. The manager accepted the apology and walked away from their table. Sylvester then shrugged his shoulders and said, "What's with all the questions? You're not ready !" Paul started begging Sylvester for a chance in a serious manner, saying, "I'll leave the bottle alone and clean up my act ! I will prove to you that you are wrong. Give me a chance, man ! Do this for me; I have been unemployed for a month now. My family has gotta eat; do this for me !" Sylvester, with a no- nonsense look, answered, "Do this for you? You want a chance is what you're asking me?" Bird had then calmed down, making his way back to their table. Sylvester then nodded his head in agreement with Paul and said," Alright." Paul in awe began to say thank you a couple times. Bird then showed up at the table and got curious and had an idea of what had happened. Bird gazed at Sylvester and said, "I don't like this. This I don't like, Sylvester; you gave him a chance, didn't you?" Sylvester then got up from his seat and patted Bird on the back, answering, "I'd do it for you." Bird then shook his head no and said, "He will disappoint you, De Nino, but what do I know?" Paul then got up and avoided eye contact with Bird and left, saying thanks again to Sylvester. Sylvester then waved at the nearest waiter to pay the bill. Sylvester and Bird left shortly after.

Later that evening at the hospital, Dean was watching baseball on TV. He then looked at the family portrait on the chair near him. He smiled, looking at Sylvester, Marie, Monica, and Renee. Dean then smiled at the thought of having a grandson.

Meanwhile at the De Nino residence, Sylvester and Paul that evening were on the phone in the kitchen talking about business. Marie was sitting at the couch in the living room, hearing their conversation while watching TV. Paul, being eager, asked, "Question, is your father selling the company?" Sylvester answered, "He did. Listen, it's getting late. Remember we have a meeting in two days ! My lawyer Connie will be there and ready." Paul then made a sarcastic comment, saying, "Will Bird be there too?" Sylvester chuckled at the remark, shaking his head, replied, "Bird won't even speak to me because of you ! All right, see you in two days and bring your lawyer too." Marie then got up and went into the kitchen. Sylvester hung up, not knowing she overheard about Bird. Marie then asked, "Bird isn't speaking to you because of Paul? What happened?" Sylvester smiled and touched her stomach answered, "All that matters to me is my family, nothing happened." They then kissed and headed to their room for bed.

Chapter 2

The Change of Heart

he next morning at 4:15 am, Sylvester woke up out of a deep sleep to a phone call from the hospital while in bed with Marie. Sylvester then reached to the bed dresser next to him and looked at the phone, seeing two missed calls from the hospital. Sylvester then answered and began to panic, hearing the news about his father. Marie then woke up concerned, hearing the conversation. The nurse from the emergency room gave Sylvester the bad news that Dean had passed this morning from heart failure. Marie then held Sylvester as he cried in thought of his father. The nurse heard and replied, "I'm sorry, Mr. De Nino. Your father seemed to have been doing well. Was he under any stress? …. Would you like to speak with Dr. Steward? …. Hello?" Sylvester then dropped the phone crying a little louder, waking up Monica. Marie, feeling his pain, began to cry, saying, "We are here ! We are here for you, we are here." Monica then left her room and knocked at their door in concern of hearing her father cry. Marie, in a sorrowful way, answered, "Come in." When Monica opened their door, she saw her parents crying and hugging each other. Marie then stretched her hand out to Monica, saying, "Grandpa is gone !" Monica then began to cry, coming to her mother. Marie, not seeing Renee said, "Tell your sister !" Monica immediately ran to Renee's room, waking her up with the sad news. Renee then hugged Monica and started to cry. Within a few minutes, the girls joined their parents. The De Nino's could not rest after hearing Dean had passed away. Sylvester later walked all around the house with thoughts on his father and the funeral.

The De Nino family agreed to have the funeral at the church Dean joined on a Saturday morning a week later. The burial service just up the road from the church. Sylvester then spoke with Dean's bishop over the phone in regards to everything. Family and close friends were informed and had called Sylvester with encouraging words. Sylvester wouldn't answer any work-related phone calls. Paul was upset, not hearing from Sylvester but wouldn't visit.

The day the funeral had happened, the church was crowded. Family and friends were there. Dean was sixty-three years old, slim and short with jet black hair. Dean was dressed in a black suit with a red tie in an opened coffin. Bird later came dressed in a suit and tie to pay his respects. Sylvester sat with his family in the front row surprised to see Bird. Bird then came to Dean's coffin, saying," Dean, gone too soon. I'm gonna miss you." Bird then walked to the back of the church, looking for a seat. More family came to the coffin, shedding tears. When Marie saw Bird, she thought to speak with him to have a better understanding after the burial service.

When the burial service was over, Marie saw Bird leaving so she met with him, saying, "Hi Bird ! Listen, I don't mean to be forward but is everything alright between you and Sylvester?" Bird smiled at Marie, looking at her stomach answered, "Paul isn't a good aim for partnership. Marie, you know this ! It was good seeing you." Bird then walked away from Marie, then came her daughters while she agreed. Marie then gazed at them, asking, "Where's your father?" The girls had no idea where Sylvester was at the time. Sylvester was with Lewis near Lewis's car being encouraged and comforted. When Sylvester finally got himself together, he met with his family and they all went home shortly after.

Two days later, the De Nino family met with Dean's executor named Robert at Dean's lawyer office in regards to Dean's will and testament and request. Dean's lawyer named Jim was looking over the will document, then handed it to Robert. Robert then reviewed the will document, smiled, and said, "I have good news." Robert glanced at everyone and read the message, leaving them speechless and in tears. After all was said and done in regards to their share of money, Robert shook Sylvester's hand and watched Marie hug her daughters still in tears. Sylvester then thought about his father and the art gallery leaving the office with his family. When the De Nino family came home, they all sat in the living room and conversed about Dean being in a better place. Sylvester, in his chair, had past thoughts of his parents raising him as an only child.

After two hours had passed, Sylvester got up from his chair and walked into the kitchen. Marie saw and joined him, asking," What's your plan? Are you still going to do the art gallery?" Sylvester glanced at Marie and answered, "Yes. I just need my space right now." Marie then realized and said, "I understand. We're here for you, hun." Sylvester then watched Marie go back into the living room with the girls.

Two weeks later one afternoon, Sylvester, at home in the living room, called Paul for a business meeting at his lawyer's office. Sylvester gave the address; they agreed to meet up at three pm in two days. When Paul had asked in regards to the name of the gallery, Sylvester thought of his wife having a love for canaries answered, "Canaries." Paul agreed with the name and said, "I have two buildings saved on my laptop. I will show you when we meet." Sylvester then spoke about the money his father had left the family, also how much he was willing to invest to make things work. Marie, at that time, had come downstairs and heard Sylvester mention the word invest. Sylvester then glanced at Marie, looking worried and waiting for him to hang up. Sylvester then says, "We'll talk later. I gotta go . ... Bye." Marie then sat down at the bottom step and again shared her feelings with Sylvester, hoping to get through to him, saying, "I have a bad feeling about this; this partnership would hurt the family !" Sylvester, feeling confused with the comment, asked, "Where is this coming from? We talked about this." Marie, out of concern, said, "It's just me talking. So, has he changed for the better?" Sylvester, judging his good spirit over the phone, answers, "I believe he has. He's still with Stephanie." Marie asked, "And, how is she?" Sylvester then shrugged his shoulders and quickly answered, "Fine, I guess." "Marie, knowing he was getting frustrated, in a calmly manner asked, "Have you thought of going into business for yourself? Wouldn't your father want it that way, love?" Sylvester heard where she was coming from and answered, "I just thought to do things differently this time around was all."

Monica and Renee had been dropped off by their friend's mother. Sylvester and Marie heard them coming to the door. Sylvester went on to say, "Tell you what, if there is a sign not to do business with Paul, then I won't. Ok?" Marie, feeling comfortable with the comment, nodding said, "Ok." Monica then opened the door with Renee, happy to be home. Marie had gotten up and they all hugged, then the girls went upstairs. Renee yelled, "JANIE'S MOM SAID

HI, MOM !" Marie then walked to Sylvester, hugging him said, "Ok." Marie then gazed at him asking, "When is your meeting with Paul?" Sylvester answers, "In two days .... See what happens, right?" Marie nodded, then walked into the kitchen to start dinner. Sylvester began to think about the meeting with Paul.

The day the meeting happened, Marie made sure that Sylvester was ready for anything. Sylvester and Marie were in the kitchen going over a few things at the kitchen table with their keys next to a mug. Marie wanted to be at the meeting but did not want confrontation with Paul. Marie, being peculiar, asked, "Have you guys come up with a name for the art gallery yet?" Sylvester laughed and says, "Canaries ! You came to mind; we agreed on the name." Marie was move by the name. They then kissed as he reached for his keys from the kitchen table. Marie watched him leave, saying, "Be safe."

When Sylvester arrived, he met and greeted Connie at the entrance. Connie asked, "Your partner is scheduled to be here too, right?" Sylvester glanced at his watch and replied, "Yes, he'll be here." They then went inside the building.

Paul, an hour later, woke up to a hangover in the apartment of his ex-girlfriend named Rita. Paul looked at his phone in bed and saw it was 2:20 pm. Rita was in the bathroom doing her hair, singing. Paul then saw three missed calls from Stephanie and a text message from Sylvester. Paul, in his boxers, got up and yelled,"RITA ! ….. HURRY UP IN THERE !" Rita heard but ignored Paul.

It then became three pm and Sylvester with Connie was wondering if Paul would show. They were in the conference room inside the law firm building. Connie, in concern for her client, asked, "Mr. De Nino, does Mr. Lagaipa understand how important this meeting is? Where is his lawyer?" Sylvester seated next to her, shaking his head out of frustration answers, "Yes. And I believe his lawyer is on the way too; let's hope." The later it got, Marie was worried for Sylvester making wrong decisions. She wouldn't text but grabbed her keys from the kitchen table. Monica and Renee were in the living room watching TV. Marie said, "I'll be back, girls." Monica watched her mother leave said, "Alright, Mom !" Renee then heard the door closed asked," Where is Mom going?" Monica shrugged her shoulders and says,"I don't know. But she looks worried." Monica and Renee continued to watch TV that afternoon.

Paul then showed up at five pm, dressed casual, drunk, and moody. Paul went into the building and found the conference room where they were. Paul and Sylvester immediately began arguing about his behavior and showing up late to a business meeting drunk. Sylvester replied, "Paul, what's wrong with you? I said three pm ! It's five pm, Paul !" Connie then got up with her purse, shaking her head at Paul.

Connie says, "This is so unprofessional. I can't work like this!" Paul looked at her and yelled, "SIT DOWN!.... WORK LIKE WHAT?" Paul then looked at Sylvester and said, "You don't need her, man!" Sylvester, in a calm manner, looked at Connie and said, "Connie, I apologize." Connie answers, "Maybe we should reschedule this meeting with a different partner. Right?" Sylvester agreed with Connie and thanked her as she headed out of the room. Sylvester, and Paul following, left the room. They continued arguing in the hallway exiting out the law firm. Sylvester, still angry around the parking lot, gazed at Paul and said, "I don't understand this at all! You begged me! What's wrong with you!?" Paul watched Connie drive off answers with rage, "What do you mean what's wrong with me? I am here, aren't I? You don't run my life." Sylvester then yelled, "PAUL, YOU DO THIS EVERY TIME!.... YOU'RE EITHER DRUNK OR OUT OF YOUR MIND!" The argument started to get real violent; lawyers outside and inside were watching. Marie was making her way driving close to the building around this time.

Paul answered in a scornful manner, "Whatever! All I want is my money. That's right! The money, De Nino!" Sylvester, being fed up, said, "You're drunk! We are not doing business together. I." Paul then cut him off and replied,"I don't need this! I'm outta here!" Sylvester watched him walk away says, "You're gonna do what you want anyhow! You know, it's even a miracle you got here Paul!" Sylvester, still upset with the situation, went back inside the building to cool off. Paul got furious and gets into his car taking off with speed. Sylvester was inside standing around the hallway. A lawyer named James came and asked if he was alright. Before Sylvester could answer, two cars had hit outside the building. The sound was like a loud thunder had crash in the parking lot. Sylvester and the lawyers rushed outside to see what had happened. Sylvester recognize the two cars were Marie's and Paul's in a total wreck.

Sylvester immediately ran over, screaming from the top of his lungs, "MARIE ! MARIE !" Sylvester then opened her door and saw she was dead, with no sign of their daughters. Blood was on her forehead and chest from the impact with a seatbelt. James was on the phone calling 911 with three lawyers gather around Sylvester as he lost it. Sylvester then looked over at the car Paul was in as the horn was sounding. Sylvester knew Paul was dead, bleeding with his head leaning on the steering wheel without a seatbelt. James was looking at the glass from her windshield and yelled, "THE AMBULANCE IS ON IT'S WAY !" Sylvester then broke down and cried, covering his face and being comforted by the lawyers. Sylvester within a few minutes called the house and Monica answered. Sylvester, at a loss for words, couldn't talk. Monica replied," Pop?.. Hello?" That day, Sylvester felt devastated and all that was left in his life was his daughters.

Sylvester then completely shut down, being burdened with the loss of his father, wife, and son. Sylvester was full of unforgiveness toward Paul's family, thoughts of his wife and unborn son left him feeling bitter. Sylvester then became overprotective of his daughters growing up. Sylvester began working for Omar's architecture company for the next ten years. In 2016, they all moved out of the old house; the girls being young adults ready for a new Chapter in their lives. Sylvester found a house in the suburbs near a beach in East Haven, Connecticut.

Monica and Renee lived together at the house Dean had left them in the suburbs of East Haven, Connecticut. Monica became an assistant manager working for a graphic design company called, Samantha's Way. Monica was short and slim with a short hairstyle. She worked with the owner named Samantha Santino hosting a meeting and supervised her coworkers, having a love for graphic arts and art in general. Monica became good friends with her coworkers Bret, Steve, and Laura at work. Renee was short and slim with long dark hair. Renee wasn't sure what she wanted to do in life after high school and later on got into a relationship with a smart, African-American named Feng Winters. Feng at the time was the lead local bouncer for a club. Feng then quit shortly after selling his house, making him financially secure and lived with Renee. Feng, since a baby, was adopted and given the name by a Chinese Christian family. Feng was the family's last name. Feng was well-built and bald with a beard. Renee then dyed her hair blonde for a different look.

On a Tuesday afternoon in late June of 2018, at Samantha's Way in East Haven, Connecticut. Bret and Steve were waiting outside Samantha's office. Rita the supervisor had told them the boss wanted to see them a few minutes ago. Rita was a middle age hip, slim, loyal woman, always dressed casual with a ponytail. Steve was a dirty blonde hipster, slim and short. Bret was shave-headed, tall and cunning. Bret and Steve shared transportation and had a habit of being late. They were worried for their jobs. Bret took a breather, then knocked at her door. Samantha, seated at her desk, said, "Come in !" Bret with Steve came in, leaving the door open and thinking the worst. Samantha was short, slim, and demanding. Samantha was dressed casually, placing her high heels on the desk. Samantha then stared at them, running her fingers throw her long, dark hair. The quietness then became awkward with the sweet smell of spices and peach in a bowl at her desk. Bret asked, "You wanted to see us?" Samantha, in a calm manner, answers, "Bret, you might be getting written up like your friend Steve. Listen …. you guys are on the edge of being fired ! Yes, due to being late." Steve, in denial, replied, "Maybe one day last week, last week?" Bret, agreeing with Steve not being honest, said, "Yeah. We've been here."

Samantha reminded them of the previous Monday, saying, "I was waiting on you two to show up for work. I found out from Monica you guys weren't here! This Tuesday you both were late again and in the copy room. I came over and caught you both clowning around. You guys are two days behind and late! This is Samantha's Way! ….You guys have a lot of call-outs and nine tardies in one month."

Steve, beginning to stress out, replied, "Samantha, I called Laura and Rita but nobody answered ! I don't believe this !" While Steve was trying to explain himself, the stock clerk named Troy who was hip and curious came around and knocked on her door. Troy looked at Samantha asked, "Samantha, you have a minute?" Samantha glanced at Troy, answering, "Not right now, Troy. Where is Rita? Tell her !" Troy nodded then left. Steve went on further and replied, "What can I do to keep my job?" Samantha got up and answers, "Come to work. You should have called me instead. That's all I ask !" Bret tried to break the tension by looking at how she was dressed and asked, "Samantha, you have a date or some other occasion? You look very nice." Steve, not going with the comment, looked away as Samantha answers, "Why thank you, Bret. Listen, bottom line is this is Samantha's Way ! You two should be keeping me happy because I am not with your actions." Bret and Steve looked down, nodding their heads in agreement with her. Samantha, hoping her message got to them, said, "Alright, get to work." Steve and Bret left her office and went into their own offices to finish the work. Three hours had passed and Bret finished half of the work. Bret left and closed his door, then checked on Steve. Bret stood by Steve's door, watching him asked, "Steve, you need help, bro?" Steve, feeling tired at the desk doing touch- ups with brochures on his laptop, answered, "I don't think I can finish today. These brochures should have been done two days ago, bro, and don't start with me !"

Bret laughed at the comment, then his phone in his back pocket started to vibrate. Rita, in the hallway, saw Bret reaching for his phone, came over, and asked, "Are you guys all set?" Bret, looking at his phone, saw a unfamiliar number and ignored the call, responding, "Steve needs more time." Steve, not in a good mood, got up with the thought of having too much work. Bret then gazed at Rita, saying, "Rita, I heard you singing the other day. I had no idea that you can sing." Rita laughed at the remark and answered, "I love to sing. I also loved art. I dated a guy ten years ago named Paul; he being a part owner wanted to hire me for singing at this art gallery called Canaries." Steve scratched his head wondered what had happened. Steve then shut the laptop off and asked, "So, why are you here?" Rita glanced at Steve and answers, "I did not know he had a wife and kid. Two weeks later, he died driving drunk and Canaries never happened. Anyhow, you guys wrap things up." Rita then walked away, doing a routine checkup. Steve, getting ready to leave with Bret, said, "The choices people make, right?" Troy, then leaving the copy and print room, saw Steve closing his door with Bret. Troy rushed over to them, saying, "Hey ! I meant to catch you both earlier ….Samantha told me to ask could you guys stay and do some overtime tonight?" Steve shook his head no and answered, "I have a life, Troy." Steve then glanced at Bret with the thought of leaving through the back door. He then mentioned it to Bret. Bret, in a sarcastic manner, replied, "Ya think !"

Troy watched them leave from the back, shaking his head and continued working. Samantha then came out her office to Laura Lopiano, the secretary, saying, "I have been looking for Monica's brochure in my office. I know I gave her the day off. Did I leave it out here?" Laura saw Samantha look at her desk answers, "I don't have it out here. Oh yeah, Bret and Steve did call out Monday. I just haven't gotten back to you." Samantha stopped looking and asked, "Have you seen Steve or Bret anywhere? I should had told them to check with me before leaving." Laura shook her head no and answers, "I haven't seen those two in about three hours. Steve LaBranche, right? Maybe they went out for a late lunch !" Samantha yelled, "RITA !" Samantha then gazed at Laura, saying," We only have one Steve here, Laura." Laura then handed her the request forms of the days she needed off. Samantha looked it over while waiting for Rita. Laura saw and quickly stashed a comedy club flyer near her phone, watching Samantha review the request form. Samantha then frowned and said, "Lopiano ! I noticed you requested Monday and Tuesday off. I'm not sure I can give you those days off. But.. let me check again before you leave. All I ask is for people to come to work !" Samantha, walking back to her office with the request form, yelled again, "RITA ! WHERE ARE YOU?" Rita then left the copy room and ran to Samantha's office to know what she wanted. Rita then stood at the door and answered, "Yes?" Samantha then sat down and leaned back, avoiding documents at her desk asked, "Where were you?" Rita answered, "I was in the copy room. My copies are still in the room." Samantha then said, "I wish Monica wasn't off. We have so much work. Let's start setting up interviews; you know what to do." Rita answered, "I will start now." Samantha then waved her away, looking over documents.

Renee and Feng arrived home from the mall that afternoon. Renee had opened the door with two shopping bags coming inside the house walking to Monica's room ready to show off the clothes she brought. Renee in her sister's room then sat down the shopping bags on the floor. Feng came inside after locking the SUV. Feng then closed the door and walked into the hallway on the phone with a friend. Monica was sitting on her bed, playing games on the phone. Renee then reached into a bag and showed off a purple shirt with a lot of glitter on it. Monica then laid her phone at the bed and reached and held up the shirt, smiling. Monica then laid the shirt down on the bed next to her, saying, "I really like this shirt. What else did you buy?" Renee then reached back into the same bag again and showed a black shirt with crazy designs and a white shirt in the same style. Monica, looking at the two shirts, said, "Hand me the black shirt." They then heard Feng laughing on the phone. Monica gazed at Renee, asking, "Renee? Who is he talking to?" Renee, not knowing, shrugged her shoulders and continued showing the clothes she bought. Renee then called out to Feng, saying, "Feng !" Feng heard then came into the room answered, "What's up, bae?" Renee held both shirts up, asking, "Which shirt do you like, the black one or white?" Feng answered, "I'm still on the phone."

Feng continued talking on the phone in the hallway. Renee sat on the bed next to Monica, saying, "We all should do something ! Hiking or shopping? Well, maybe not shopping because I don't wanna hear Feng say his feet hurt and it's my fault." Monica laughed at the remark and answered, "We shopped three days ago and you, my dear, shopped today. I don't think we ever went hiking before. That would be different for a change but where?" Renee answers, "What would be different for a change is you meeting a nice guy, just saying. Monica, you haven't dated in a year." Monica got up and removed her earrings and, before answering, looked across in Renee's room and saw their mother's painting. Monica then walked into Renee's room and thought about their mother. Renee then followed and stood next to Monica, saying, "I miss Mom. I remember when people would get in our family business, Mom would say, 'Canaries are talking or bunch of canaries they are !'" Monica smiled at the remark, saying, "That's Mom for ya ! She had that beautiful, long, dark hair, slim and short like me." Renee laughed at the comment, saying,"You know you look like Mom, Chi Chi, but I have her hair in blonde though."

Feng then got off the phone and saw the girls were in Renee's room. Feng looked over at the painting and, out of being curious, asked, "What's up?" Monica smiled, then sat on her sister's bed and answers, "I just miss my mother. Say? Have you met your mother "Rachel, yet?" Feng gazed at Monica, then shook his head no and answered, "I'm with the Feng family." Renee smiled and said, "I remember you asking me out. That is after you and what's his name made the news a few months back." Feng answers, wAs beautiful as you are, most guys would want a chance with you. I didn't understand Chase." Monica, not knowing what they were talking about, asked, "Who is Chase?" Renee glanced at Monica, lost in the conversation, and using sarcasm answers, "A cheater ! Anyhow, are we going hiking?" Feng and Monica thought on the question that afternoon.

Later that afternoon, Bret was leaning on his truck with Steve, tired from work. They hung out in downtown New Haven at a shopping plaza called Mikey's, looking at beautiful women shop. Steve, having a question, looked at Bret and asked, "Hey Bret. You ever wonder where your life is taking you?" Bret answered, "To tell you the truth, I don't think on it, never have." Steve looked around and nodded his head, knowing the conversation wasn't going anywhere. Bret then remembered a girl Steve was talking to asked, "So, what ever happen to that girl you ask out?" Steve, thinking on the comment, answered, "Last week, right?" Bret began laughing and said, "Yeah. Was it a girl from work?" Steve frowned at the remark, remembering the girl answers, "No, not from work. That girl got fired. Green eyes?" Bret says, "Green eyes and long, dark hair. You spoke about her all last week, what happen?" Steve answers, "You're talking about Sandy? Dude, she is trouble. I almost got into a fight with a big man because of her. Some money from his pocket fell, and the guy turn and saw Sandy take it. This happened at the only gas station on Cherry Road. I couldn't beat that guy. Sandy tried to hide behind me and instigate." Bret laughed at the situation, then their friend from high school, Carmen Lagaipa, was driving into the plaza. Carmen saw and park next to them. Carmen was the son of Paul Lagaipa. He was twenty-two years old.

Carmen gets out of his red sports car, dressed casually and wearing dark shades. Carmen walked over to the guys, greeting them with a handshake. Carmen says, "Hey, you guys look tired ! Long time no see, what going on?" They both responded that they were fine. Steve, being curious, says, "I'm exhausted, how are you, man? Where do you work at now by the way?" Bret then gazed at the sport car, amazed, and asked, "Carmen, how do you do it, man?" Carmen, smirking at the comment, answered, "I'm doing good. Bret, you like it? I am a manager at a waste corporate office on Webster Avenue in East Haven. I like that my office is on the first floor and were doing good."

Two, young, attractive blondes, dressed casually, came out of a clothing store and looked at the red sports car and Carmen. Carmen, watching the ladies walk away to their cars, asked, "Where are you guys working now?" Bret answered, "Samantha's Way !" It's a graphic design company in East Haven. Steve and I make do over there." Carmen then looked back at them and noticed that they weren't happy, ask, "Are you guys doing anything Friday?" Bret, thinking on his work schedule, answered, "Friday. I don't think I work Friday." Steve laughed at the comment made and replied, "Bret and I have the same schedule; should be off, man." Carmen then heard and saw the two blondes talking about him. Carmen looked back again at the fellas and says, "Come down to my office. I'm having a party plus a sweet opportunity for you both to make some money. Who better then you both, right? So, what do you say?" They both agreed to come to the party Friday.

Steve chuckled at the comment and said, "I see you're downtown. I could use a break. I want to hear more about this opportunity though. Are we talking about a manager position or ....?" Carmen answered, "I'm the boss. Come down to my office and we will talk about everything." Bret and Steve were excited and couldn't wait until Friday. Carmen, being distracted by the two blondes, said, "Talk to you guys later, ok?" Carmen then met with the ladies, introducing himself and saying, "Hey, what's happening ! I'm Carmen !" The girls felt comfortable and laughed, giving their names. One answered, "Hi, I'm Angela. Were you checking me out back there?" They both laughed at the remark. The other girl answered, "Ivana." Ivana asked, "Is that your car?" Carmen, lusting after them, answered, "Yeah, that my car. Hey, take my number?" The girls laughed at Carmen, reaching for his phone from the back pocket. Ivana asked, "Which one?" Carmen smiled, then glanced at Bret and Steve, forgetting to ask for their number. Carmen yelled, "BRET, STEVE ! I GOTTA GET YOUR NUMBERS ! ... GIVE ME A MINUTE !" Steve then glanced at Bret, saying, "It's gotta be the car, bro . ... This dude was really distracted." Bret, being funny, watching the girls flirt with Carmen answered, "Ya think !"

It then became the evening time. Renee was with Feng in her room, relaxing. Renee began to check her phone, walking around her mother's painting. Feng sat at the bed, thinking about college. Renee stopped and gazed at Feng, saying, "Feng?" Feng looked at Renee, waiting for her to continue on and answered, "Yeah?" Renee looked at Feng, about to focus deep in thought again. She wondered what was on his mind and asked, "Are you ok?" Feng answered "I just got something on my mind." Renee got curious and asked, "What's on your mind? You can talk to me, you know." Feng smiled at the remark and answered, "College. I'm thinking about going to college." Renee then sat next to Feng, rubbing his back and saying, "You sound like my father, like business-minded, if that makes any sense." Feng got up and answered, "Really? No. Years back, I was distracted and had broken up with my ex and well … you know the rest." Renee, looking at the floor, said, "Yeah, I do."

Monica, from the kitchen, walked to Renee's room with her phone, telling them she received a text message saying Dad was here. Renee then got up and told Feng she would be right back. She met up with Monica in the hallway. The girls then walked out the house and met with their father standing near the front porch, hugging. He was parked behind Monica's car. Sylvester was dressed casually, 6 feet tall, bald with a goatee. Renee like what he was wearing and asked, "So, how's everything, Pop? You look nice."

Sylvester smiled at them and answered, "Fine, how's my girls doing?" Monica said, "Good, Pop ! Feng is inside." Sylvester nodded his head and said, "So, I have good news." The girls waited for him to continue. He then said, "I found a building for our art gallery; the art gallery ten years ago I should had put together !" Renee, amazed at the comment, said, "Wow ! This is big, Pop ! What more can I say? I !" … Monica, being curious, interrupted and asked, "What's the name going to be?" Sylvester smiled and replied, "Marie's Canaries."

Sylvester went on to say, "We will all sit down and talk Monday about this when I come back. I'll be busy all week. I have a lot of ideas and I want your ideas as well. This is a family business, you know." The girls agreed to a family meeting. Monica, in thought of her schedule, slowly answered, "Monday is fine. Today is Tuesday so I don't have to hear Rita's name being yelled all day until the following Monday." Renee, making sure she understood the remark, asked, "Wait? You're off until Monday is what you're saying?" Monica answered, "Yes. So, a Monday dinner then?" Sylvester nodded and said, "Yes, let's talk about this at dinner. I know we usually don't talk about business at dinner. Also, tomorrow is my last day working for Omar." Renee and Monica were excited for their father. Renee, with the thought of hiking, said, "Pop, tomorrow we are going hiking !" Sylvester then zoned out for a bit and answered, "It sound like fun, love." Monica took notice that he zoned out and looked down, so she asked, "You ok, Pop?"

Sylvester glanced at Monica and said, "I'm still having thoughts of your mother being four months pregnant; my father selling his architecture company before passing; him leaving ten million for the family, then Paul's death." Sylvester was grieved. His daughters then hugged him in comfort. Monica looked at her father and said, "This didn't just affect you, Pop, but the family. We had to forgive Paul too. I am happy you're moving forward in opening the art gallery in Mom's honor." Renee, wanting her father to hang out with them, said, "Come inside, Pop, and relax !" Renee gazed at Monica, looking down at her phone asking, "Chi Chi, are you cooking tonight or …?" Monica, being funny, answered, "Renee, I don't recall you doing any food shopping !" Renee, walking inside the house with them, closed the door and said, "Chi Chi, I am sure this is your week to have done the food shopping." Sylvester laughing at them, scratching his head with the thought of no food in the house. Sylvester looked to the kitchen and said, "We're Italian. How is there no food in this house?" Renee shrugged her shoulders, avoiding eye contact and answered, "Beats me. I told Monica to go food shopping."

Sylvester then came more into the living room with Monica and saw a portrait of him and Marie standing outside their house in the eighties. Sylvester said, "WOW ! You guys have this in here?" Monica laughed and answered, "Yeah. What year was this picture, Pop? You had hair." Sylvester looked at her and said, "Real funny, Monica. It was 1989. This picture; now that's a thing of beauty !" Sylvester then sat at the kitchen table, talking with everyone for a few hours, then went home for the evening.

Chapter 3

Carmen's Plan

The next morning at Carmen's office, Ben was talking about a woman he met. Ben, sitting near the desk, looked at Carmen seated at the desk. Ben said, "I was talking to this skinny blonde named Roxy, right? Maybe one day I will take you guys out with me to meet some real hot ones. Anyhow, I ...." Victor stood next to Carmen, interrupting to say, "Not a good idea. I don't like fast woman. Carmen doesn't either; not a good idea." Ben undermined the comment and went on to say, "So, I am talking to this girl, right? So, what happens? Roxy invites me over and ...." Ben then stopped and gazed at Victor, making a weird face deep in thought. Ben quickly asked, "What? What is it?" Victor looked at Ben and said, "Think I know her. I know a skinny blonde name Roxy that lives near the beach in West

Haven." Ben, amazed but curious, asked, "Yeah, you know her?" Victor, feeling awkward, looked away and answered," Know her !" Carmen then interrupted by raising his hand and yelling, "ZIP IT !" Victor noticed that Carmen had been quiet all morning so he asked, "What is it, boss? Not for nothing but you been quiet all morning." Carmen glanced at Ben and answered, "I have an idea. A very rich idea, you guys." Ben, waiting for Carmen to continue on, asked, "You're saying rich? How rich, boss?" Carmen, knowing he had their attention, answered, "The De Nino family ! My father told me about that family and how he would've become a part owner in the business."

Victor came closer and got anxious, asking, "What's the plan, boss?" Carmen then looked at the door closed and back at the fellas, answering, "You two are just like me in a way, alright. We keep this between us, fellas." Ben and Victory agreed by nodding their heads. Carmen then leaned forward in his chair, saying, "Their father's name is Sylvester. We kidnap one or both of his daughters. I might need two extra guys to be my eyes and I believe I know who to ask." Ben became curious and asked, "Who? And what if they say no? Also, where and what do these girls look like?"

Carmen stared at Ben on the remarks made. He then goes into the top drawer and gazed at his gun, next to an old photo of Paul standing with Sylvester and his two daughters outside an ice skate center. Carmen then put the photo on his desk so they would know the girls' features and gave their names. Carmen then said, "Five million will be the ransom. This family has money." Victor was left speechless. Ben excited said, "This sounds too easy, boss. I'm in. This wouldn't be the first time I robbed someone." Victor spoke up and said, "Me too. I'm in." Carmen then said, "My mother ran into Monica two days ago shopping. She's still in East Haven from what I was told but where right?" Ben said, "I was meaning to ask you; were they still in the area? Their father looks familiar. I wish your mother had ask her then, boss." Carmen said, "I agree. The two men are Bret and Steve, jocks that I grew up with is all. I don't think they would say no; I know these two."

Carmen then planned everything out and started with where he remember they lived. Carmen then wrote down the old address for Victor to stalk. Victor left immediately as he was told and drove to the old address. When Victor arrived and parked in front of the house, he saw the Lox's family name written on the mailbox. Victor got out of the car, seeing a truck parked outside the garage. He looked around the area and saw no one, then came to the door and started knocking in search for the girls. Mr. Lox was seated on the couch, watching TV in the living room and heard the knocking. He got up to see who it was. Mr. Lox came to the door and asked, "Who is it?" Victor lied, claiming to be a cousin of the De Nino family, yelling, "IT'S YOUR COUSIN, MARIO ! ....HOW'S EVERYONE?" Mr. Lox had frowned at the comment, opening the door, looking at this lean, tall man with short, dark hair and a goatee answered, "I think you have the wrong address, my friend." Victor then asked, "Did they move already? Did you know them?" In their conversation, Mr. Lox mentioned he'd been living there for a few months; the Mckoy family lived there before his family. Mr. Lox made known that he never met the De Nino family, and that he should ask his neighbors. Victor agreed and walked back to his car, not wanting to be suspicious. He then sat in the car, about to call Carmen. Victor then received a call from Ben, answering, "What's up?" Ben asked, "They still live there or what?" Victor said, "No. How are you making out? I was gonna call Bossman and let him know." Ben answered, "Making my round. I was hoping they'd still live there so we could wrap this thing up. Alright." Ben then hung up; Victor immediately called Carmen.

Ben drove around, asking people about the De Nino family. Ben was lying to people in the area close to the old address. He claimed to be visiting friends. Ben, an hour later, needed a break. He then went to a coffee shop for a cup of coffee. Ben went inside, looking at a few people sitting at tables drinking coffee. The front cashier saw and asked, "What can I get for you?" Ben ordered a small, black coffee. After he received and paid for the coffee, he asked,"Hey, are there any customers or employees with the last name De Nino that live around here? I'm Mitch by the way. A Monica or Renee; they're sisters, not really sure which one works here."

The cashier shook his head no and answered,"No sir. A friend of yours, right? You don't have their number?" Ben smiled at the cashier, looking at people coming inside, then stood behind him. Ben looked back at the cashier and answered, "Yeah, a friend. Last we spoke, I forgot to get her number. Can you believe that ! In fact, there is a baby shower coming up." The cashier, a little confused, then walked away and asked the manager making coffee near the drive-thru. The manager answered, "Yeah. One comes here all the time. She doesn't work here but her name is Monica." The manager then turned around and saw Monica with her window down, receiving an ice coffee from the drive-thru. The cashier said,"In fact, that's her in the white SUV leaving the drive-thru now in the back seat."

The cashier, not knowing what to do, asked, "Should I tell him?" Ben heard their conversation surprise. He rushed out the coffee shop and accidently spill his coffee into a customer's shirt running outside. The customer got angry and curse him out, drying himself. Ben ran to his car and drove off, almost hitting a car passing him in the parking lot. The cashier and manager saw everything. The cashier got upset and said, "He almost hit that car ! Was the baby shower that important?" The manager then shrugged her shoulders and continued working. Feng was driving his white SUV with Renee in the passenger seat. Monica was in the back seat, ready to hike.

Renee relaxed and looked at them said, "It's very cool and sunny right now. I can't wait to experience what nature has to offer. The green way should lead us to the beautiful river view, historical sites as well."Feng smiled at the remark and answered, "I forgot to pick up a gun. We gotta make one more stop." Renee frowned at what was said and responded, "You are not killing anything, mister!" Feng, laughing at Renee's expression, said, "It was a joke, love, you know. Joke." Monica, holding her ice coffee, yelled, "TURN THE RADIO ON PLEASE!" Renee then turned the radio on and left it on the nineties station. They all were singing to whatever had come on, full of joy and not noticing they were being followed into Guilford. Ben then reached for his phone and called Carmen while driving. Carmen was standing outside his office. Receiving the phone call, he said, "Hello?" Ben answered, "I found them and now I am following them!" Carmen amazed asked, "You found them already?" Ben, trying not to get too close, answered, "Yeah, at a coffee shop." Carmen said, "Stay with them and use your phone to get a picture of their license plate, what they're driving, and what they look like now. Don't make a move until I tell you!" Ben, making a left turn following them, said, "Alright."

They finally arrived at the forest park, and after paying a fee and parking, Renee then turned the radio off. Feng, Monica, and Renee got out looking around, then stretched their legs. Ben used his phone, taking pictures, wearing dark shades, and parked out of sight. The three of them, having no idea where to start in the woods, began to walk and glance around and saw no people around. Feng glanced at the girls asked, "You girls have never been hiking before at all, right?" Renee, reaching for his hand, answered, "No, Monica and I join the Girls Scouts before ! Well, how hard can it be? Right?" Renee then saw a path leading into the woods so she pointed in the direction, saying, "That looks like our starting point. It's hiking time !" As they started to walk in that direction, Monica's phone started to ring so she answered. "Hello?" Bret from his office quickly responded, "Hey, it's Bret. Listen, Samantha is on my case about calling out. I need your help with work because I am like two weeks behind." Monica frowned out of frustration, saying, "How are you two weeks behind? Oh, that's right.. Because you keep calling out ! You're asking me for help, buddy …. I am on vacation right now."

Bret then said, "The reasons I called you was because I can't come in tomorrow." Monica gazed at the trees, shaking her head and disappointed on the phone. She then looked at Renee waiting. Monica then answered, "Dude, you're gonna get fired !" Renee, looking around the forest, replied, "Chi Chi ! Yo, Chi Chi ! I'm getting bored." Feng sarcastically said, "I wanna go home." Monica, still on the phone, said, "I am off for a few days."Bret then began to panic over work and replied, "A few days.. what day is it, Wednesday?" Monica, not wanting to hear any excuses, interrupted and said, "Listen, I gotta go. Stop calling out, Bret." Monica then hung the phone up, staring at them for being rude and said, "Ya know ... You guys are something else !" Renee, looking at the woods, started to panic. She then saw the bushes moving near them and said, "Feng, I've no clue what awaits us. I'm talking animals, you know !" Monica laughed at the remark. She then gazed at Feng, saying, "Feng, you should had seen this one. Renee would avoid the woods all the time as a Girl Scout." Feng laughed at the comment. Monica stood and looked around the woods, then back at the SUV and said,"Alright, I am not feeling this hike at all." Feng smiled and asked, "Would you feel safe if we had a gun?" Monica frowned at the mention. Renee then crossed her arms and yelled, "WHAT DID I SAY !" Feng then walked away and said, "Your pops should have taken you both hunting or something. I mean you both were Girl Scouts but never went in the woods?" They then decided to go back to the SUV and return home.

When they got inside the SUV, Monica looked over and saw a handsome guy in a car wearing a green shirt and shades. He was talking with a man that stood near him out-side the park. Monica asked, "Who's the cutie in the car?" Renee then focused on what Monica was talking in terms of what she saw and answered, "Beats me." Feng replied, "What a wasted trip. This was your idea, Renee, just saying." Renee, with her hands up, aggravatedly yelled, "OK! OK! .... NEXT TIME YOU PICK A PLACE TO GO TO ! ..... I WOULDN'T

EXACTLY CALL EAST HAVEN TO GUILFORD A TRIP BUT WHAT DO I KNOW !" Renee then looked at Monica in the back seat, then went on to say, "By the way, it's your turn to go food shopping, Chi Chi." Pop said yesterday, being sarcastic, "We're Italian. How is there no food in the house?" Monica frowned at the comment and glanced at Feng, yelling, "FENG PLEASE, WILL YOU TELL HER TO SHUT UP?" Feng ignored Monica and drove off.

Carman was the guy in the car talking to Ben about the next step reviewing the pictures taken by phone. Carmen then told Ben to follow them and see where they lived. Carmen, with a serious look, again said, "Don't make any move until I tell you." Ben went to his car, saying, "Yes, boss."

While Feng was driving, Renee gazed at him and, with a question, she asked, "Feng?" Feng made a left turn and answered, "Yeah?" Renee then asked, "What was Nia Yung like?" Feng looked at her being curious and asked, "Why?" Renee stared at him, awaiting an answer. He looked at the road, said, "She was beautiful but distant." Renee, not understanding, asked, "Distant like..?" Feng, looking at a blue sports car in the other lane passing by, then answered, "Nia went through a lot of abuse, so she had trust issues." Renee understood, then glanced at him again asked, "Did she meet your folks?" Feng gazed back at Renee and answered, "Yes. And don't worry; you will too." Renee then smiled, reaching for his hand and said, "I hope they like me." Feng smiled at the remark and said, "You? ….They will love you. Chi Chi, not sure they will." Monica, ignoring the comment, moved up and got in between them, saying, "I hate to interrupt you two but can you please turn the radio on?" Renee then turned the radio on to a station playing nothing but the hits from the nineties and 2000s until they got home. Soon as they arrived home, Ben, keeping his distance, drove away, now knowing where they lived.

Meanwhile, Sylvester was at his job in the meeting room alone with Omar, his boss. They were conversating on his last day there about him opening up the art gallery. Omar, holding a glass of water, stood and said, "Listen, my doors are always open to you. Your father, you, and I go back so this isn't easy for me." Sylvester, seated at the meeting table, glanced at him and answered, "This art gallery is heavy on my heart. My girls are helping me with this whole idea, Omar. I thank you for being there for me." Omar got curious and asked," This is just you, no partner, right?" Sylvester stared at the table for a few seconds and answered, "That's right; no partner. The way it should have been. Was Lewis working today?" Omar said, "He requested today off; he must have forgot today was your last day here." Sylvester got up and hugged Omar farewell. After they hugged, Omar watched Sylvester walk to the door and said, "Listen, if you ever need my help, let me know, man." Sylvester glanced at Omar, nodding his head, then opened and closed the door. When Sylvester walked the halls, his co-workers in their office saw him and all stood from their desks. They all gave a round of applause, knowing the history. Omar then came out of the meeting room and stood by the door with his arms crossed, smiling at Sylvester. He then clapped with everyone. Sylvester wished his daughters were there to see this happen. Omar then came to him and asked," Did ya have lunch yet?" Sylvester shook his head no and said, "I had it in mind to celebrate with my daughters later on." Omar said, "Come on; let's have lunch together. You'll catch up with them … please." Sylvester then agreed and left with Omar for lunch that afternoon.

Later that afternoon, at the De Nino residence, Feng was in the bathroom around the mirror on the phone with his father Lo about introducing Renee to them. Renee and Monica were in the kitchen, chatting about the art gallery and finishing dinner. Lo stood at the living room of his home, looking at the family pictures on the wall and asked, "How's everything?" Feng looked at himself in the mirror and answered, "Things are a lot better than the way they used to be. How's Mom?" Lo touched a picture of him and his wife and answered, "She's fine. When we were in Florida, she kept asking me did you eat?" Lo then got curious and continued on to say, "What were you doing around that time?" Feng laughed at the question, then heard the ladies' conversation getting loud answers. "Avoiding trouble, really? You remember it was on the news. Officer Chase, Nia, and I lived out of that war zone." Lo remembered and said,

"That's right; it was nothing but the grace of God that pro-
tected you all." Lo started walking into the kitchen, saying,
"See you tomorrow." Feng scratching his bread, leaving
the bathroom, answered, "See you tomorrow." Feng then
hung up and went into the kitchen with the girls.

Feng looked at the food being cooked placing his phone at
the table says, "Something smells good in here . …. What is
it?" Monica made macaroni and cheese with baked chicken.
Renee, sitting at the kitchen table, answered, "Macaroni
and cheese with baked chicken." Feng, being curious,
asked, "Renee, how come you're never cooking?" Renee
sarcastically answered, "Well, how come you're always on
the phone? I did help, Chi Chi." Feng smiled at the remark,
taking a seat at the kitchen table, knowing she was rubbed
the wrong way. In a kind tone voice, he asked, "Would
you like to meet my folks tomorrow morning?" Monica
stood around the stove and glanced at Renee's expression.
Renee, stunned at the comment and almost at a loss for
words, answered, "I'd be honored ! What are they like? I
mean, will they like me?" Feng reached for her hand and
said, "You'll be fine." Monica smiled at them and said, "Tell
me how it goes."

Monica looked at Feng and went on to say, "Feng, Renee
told me your ex was involved in a gang or something?" Feng
glanced at Monica and answered, "Her brother was ! She
hid our relationship from him and we got caught at a party

is what happened." Monica understood and looked at her sister and said, "I see. Renee has no shame; she doesn't go around lying and hiding the truth." Monica then turned the stove off, opened and closed the cabinet for plates and cups, and said, "Let's eat." The three of them filled their plates and sat down, enjoying dinner with cherry sodas. Within ten minutes, Renee thought about their father asked, "Isn't today Pop's last day at work?" Monica nodded yes, then gazed at Feng enjoying his food. Renee then said, "I'm surprised he hasn't called yet."

Monica had gotten eager with another question for Feng so she asked, "Feng. Did that gang make trouble for you?" Feng glanced at Monica after swallowing his food and answered, "No." Monica, wanting to know more, says, "Oh come on, you gotta tell me !" Renee frowned at her sister and said, "Feng, don't mind her." Feng gazed at Monica and replied, "Some are dead and the rest are in jail. Officer Chase helped me with the trouble."

Monica smiled at them and said, "Well, I am glad you guys found each other." Renee, being funny, glanced at Feng and said, "Feng, Monica is in need of a man. She hasn't dated in like a year. Can you believe that?" Monica, not liking the remark, shouted, "I AM NOT DESPERATE IS ALL ! …. THAT'S MY CHOICE, YOU KNOW; NOBODY LIKES A HEARTBREAK!" Feng nodded, agreeing with Monica saying, "Renee, she is right." Renee, watching her sister get up from the table to put her plate away, said, "I apologize, Chi Chi. So tomorrow, could you help me pick an outfit out for the Fengs?" Monica got excited and agreed to help in the morning. Shortly after they ate, everyone went to sleep that night.

Renee and Monica the next morning, around 11:30 am, were going through Renee's closet, throwing outfits left and right on the bed. Renee, at the late minute, looking at all her clothes, said, "I should have started this last night." Monica then held up a royal purple dress and asked, "You wanna try this on?" Renee glanced at the dress and shook her head no. Monica then took a breather and sat at the bed, watching Renee in aggravation look at clothes and say, "This shouldn't be hard at all. I understand giving the first impression ! Let me ask you this, and do not think on the Fengs." Monica had Renee's full attention, then continued on to say, "Renee, what do you want to wear? You're gonna want to be you, right?" Renee stopped and thought on the comment, answering, "You know what; you're right. Clearly I wasn't thinking." Feng then pulled up in the SUV at the house and blew the horn while checking his phone and waiting. Renee heard the horn and began to panic, yelling, "HE'S HERE ALREADY?" Monica laughed while helping Renee put an outfit together. After an hour, Renee came out of the front door, closing it with a ponytail and wearing a yellow dress with accessories and a peach perfume scent. Feng saw her, then got out of the SUV. He walked over and opened the door on the passenger side, liking her outfit and saying, "Your dress changed my whole feeling. I know it was an hour but I can't get mad." Renee smiled at the remark. While getting inside, she said, "Thanks. Monica helped me pick this out." After closing her door, he rushed to get back inside the vehicle and drove off, ready to meet his family.

Monica stood around her mirror, ready to leave in a pink summer dress with accessories and dark shades, with the thought being always look your best. Monica, with her purse, walked out of the house, ready to shop. Victor had just parked across their house, ready to watch. Monica then locked the front door and went to her car. She started the car up and left, backing up from the garage. Monica then made a left turn. Victor watched and followed her.

Monica then arrived and parked to the left side of a corner store called Vinnie C's. She put her shades on top of her head, going inside the store with her purse. Victor then parked across the street, watching and calling Carmen. Carmen, seated in his office, looking at documents with his phone near the desk, then received a phone call showing the name Victor. Carmen saw and picked up, saying, "Yes." Victor, waiting for her to come out, answered, "I have good news, boss ! One of his daughters is out food shopping ! You want me to grab her now?" Carmen, impressed, got up from his seat and said, "No ! Is she alone and what market?" Victor looked up at the store sign and answered, "She is alone at a corner store half the size of a supermarket called

Vinnie C's on White Street." Carmen looked at his watch and said, "Wait for me there." Victor saw and lusted after a woman dressed casually going inside the market and answered, "Alright boss." Carmen hung up, then paged and told his secretary to hold all of his phone calls until he came back. He then rushed out of his office. Monica, while shopping, began to have thoughts about Renee meeting the Feng family, hoping everything was going well.

Meanwhile at the Feng residence, they all were talking in the living room. Feng was talking with his father, Lo; Renee was with his mother named Polly. Renee felt a little over-dressed, seeing everyone wearing jeans and T-shirts but counted it all joy. Polly was short, slim, elegant, and kind with long, dark hair. Polly looked at Renee and, out of being anxious, asked, "How did you meet my son?" Renee, looking at the family pictures to the left of the wall, answered, "It's a long story, Mrs. Feng." Polly stared at her, waiting for an answer. Renee took notice and went on to say, "Let's just say by a mutual friend. A very bad, mutual, cheating friend." Polly, not liking the cheating part, out of concern rubbed her back said, "Oh dear !" Renee then raised both her hands in an expressive way, saying, "I'm ok, really. So, I hear your husband is a pastor?" Polly, learning her character, answered, "Yes, he is. My husband and I do ministry." Polly then gazed at her long, blonde hair and outfit and asked, "Where are you from?" Renee glanced at Polly and said, "East Haven. My roots are from Venice, Italy, but I am second generation in America." Lo Feng was lean, short, brave, and God-fearing, with short, dark hair. Lo smiled at the ladies conversing. He then looked at his son and asked, "Does she treat you good?" Feng walked with his father into the kitchen and answered, "Yeah, she does. She's nothing like what I was dealing with before."

Lo, being curious, asked, "Did you find a college yet?" Feng shook his head no and replied, "I'll find one; it's not that hard . …. Dad, how's Uncle Ken?" Lo answered, "Good, good. He visited not too long ago and asked about you." Lo then took a seat at the kitchen table and said, "You see yourself having a future with her?" Feng smiled at the comment and, taking a seat next to his father, answered, "Yes I do. We spoke about me going to college already." Lo smiled at Renee in the living room. He then looked at Feng and said, "I like her son. Is she a Christian?" Feng laughed at the remark and answered, "I believe so. I don't think she's Catholic." Polly then came over with Renee and said, "Come eat, everyone. I made lunch. Come, come." Polly told Renee to take a seat so she sat next to Feng, looking all over the kitchen area.

Polly gathered plates from a cabinet for everyone and placed them down at the counter, then she reached for spoons and forks in another cabinet close to a coffee machine. Feng wondering what was smelling good, looked at his mother, asked, "Mom, whatcha cook?" Polly then took a plate to the stove and answered, "Beef stew !" Lo then whispered in Feng's ear, "I can tell your mother likes her already. I'm ready to eat." Polly handed her husband a plate full of beef stew with brown rice. Renee then rested her head on Feng's shoulder and said, "What a lovely family." Feng then asked, "What's Chi Chi up to?" Renee answered, "She didn't say." They looked at each other, then kissed. Polly saw and got excited for them, making plates for everyone.

Monica was still inside the store around the sauce area in aisle four at that time. She was looking for the right sauce in the middle of the bottom shelf. She then picked up a medium size can to see if it was needed before placing it in the cart. She then heard a loud, smooth male voice and recognized it was Bird. Bird was arguing with his wife named Linda about not taking the trash out and said, "Yeah, yeah, yeah. You don't have to remind me every two seconds to take the trash out !" Linda, with the hand shopping cart, not liking the comment gave an attitude answered, "You wanna do this here?" Linda was short, lean, and watchful with long, brunette, curly hair. Bird ignored Linda, looked away, and saw Monica in the next aisle. Bird smirked, then went over to Monica, using sarcasm and saying, "Hey, it's Monica !" Linda saw Monica and walked over to her. They all greeted with a kiss on the cheek. Monica glanced at them, saying, "Hey Bird ! Linda, what's doing?"

Linda, liking what she was wearing, answered, "I'm doing fine. Monica, I like your dress." Monica smiled at the remark. Linda looked at Bird and continued on, saying, "I dragged him with me to get some fresh air and good tomato sauce." Monica laughed at the remark, saying, "I thought I was the only one that knew about the sauce here." Bird, being curious, asked, "How's your father?" Before she could answer, Bird told Linda he dated Marie months before Sylvester. Bird then gazed at Monica, saying, "I could had been your father." Monica sarcastically replied, "Which is why you and my father don't get along, Bird! You cheated on my mother, remember? My mother told me all about it." Bird looked away, avoiding eye contact, knowing it was the trust. He then stared at Monica, asking, "Is that what she told you?" Linda glanced at them, staring at each other and, feeling the pressure, she quickly asked, "Monica, how you been?" Monica then put the can inside her shopping cart and answered, "I've been good. Enjoying my time off and such." Bird gazed at Linda, cuddling her from behind. And after kissing her on the cheek, she smiled, saying, "Bird, behave."

Bird then whispered in her ear, saying, "You're my number one, my one and only." Monica then walked away from them, saying, "It was nice seeing you both." They laughed, watching Monica leave. Bird answered, "Yeah. You too, Monica." Monica went to the checkout counter and paid the cashier for the groceries, using a credit card, which led to three bags. Monica then placed the three bags back into the cart. She got on the phone, putting the cart away near the entrance. She called Renee while leaving the store, carrying out three bags and her purse with one arm. Renee asked, "Chi Chi, where are you?" Monica answered, "Vinny V's, shopping!" Monica then walked out with the groceries. Carmen saw and came over, asking, "Miss, you need help?" Monica saw a handsome, young man talking to her. She told Renee she'd call back, then answered, "Hmmm. What did you say?" Carmen, with a warming smile, asked again, "You need help? You're using just one arm for three bags and a purse?" Monica smiled at Carmen and answered, "I could use your help." Carmen then grabbed all the bags. Monica couldn't get over how handsome he was and asked, "Were you waiting on someone or..?" Carmen watched a car go by. He then gazed back at Monica and answered, "I just got to the entrance; forgot my list of items inside my car. I saw you needed help." They then walked over to her car. He looked at Monica again and said, "Wait a minute? De Nino?" Monica then unlocked her car and waited for him to continue but he didn't so she answered, "Maybe, who are you?" He chuckled and said, "Carmen Lagaipa, I believe I saw you at the forest park in Guilford . .... How are you?"

Monica watched him put all the bags inside her car, remembering him says, "I remember you and your father ! So, the guy I saw in a car at the park was you? . .... My father spoke a lot about Paul; they were buds." After he put the bags away, he came over to Monica and asked, "So, where do you live now? Are you still in East Haven? I work as a credit consulate over at Plain Road. The people over there, I tell ya …. but it's a job." Monica laughed and answered, "My sister and I are on Bloom Street now. And my father lives in East Haven too. You know, it's been years since I've seen you around. Are you still around here?" Carmen looked at her dress and answered, "Yeah. You know those apartments on Cherry Hill in New Haven? I live over there." Carmen took notice that she couldn't stop staring at him so he said, "I don't mean to be forward but we should catch up sometime. Nice dress by the way." Monica began to blush and answered, "Yeah, we should." Carmen then pulled out his cell phone from his back pocket and asked, "What's your number?" Monica smiled at the comment and said, "I'm free tomorrow night, which is Friday night." They then exchanged numbers and he knew he had her where he wanted her. Carmen asked, "What time tomorrow night? You know what? … … Call me; I gotta make a run real quick. … Ok?" Monica answered, "I'll call you tomorrow !" Carmen took two steps back and said, "I'm looking forward to tomorrow then." Carmen then began walking away and she yelled, "ALRIGHT ! … I'LL CALL YOU TOMORROW !" Carmen then crossed the street, going to Ben still watching in his car. Carmen looked back at Monica opening her car door, then met with Ben. Carmen softly said, "We will make the move tomorrow and kidnap them both . …. Call Victor. I want you and Victor to meet me at the dinner this evening on Park Ave." Ben replies, "Gotcha." Ben watched Carmen leave, parked two cars in front of him. Then came a stunning, young lady in a black sports car, parking behind Ben.

Ben, in lust, immediately got out of his car and walked up to the woman. The young lady got out of the car with a purse. She turned around and saw Ben coming her way. Ben smiled at her and said, "What a beauty. I had to come over and say something to ya. Right?" The lady started blushing at the comment. Ben then introduce himself, saying, "I'm Ben by the way." She felt comfortable with his presence and answered, "I'm Lisa." Ben, loving her green eyes and long, dark, curly hair, then saw a small heart tattoo on her neck. Ben asked, "You look Italian. Are you Italian?" Lisa smiled at what was said and answered, "One hundred percent. My full name is Lisa Lombardi." Ben, liking the conversation, replied, "I'm Italian also. Ben Ricci. You from around here? What's your number?" Ben handed her his phone. She then typed her number in, smiling. Lisa then handed him back the phone, saying "I like your confidence. Call me !" Ben watched Lisa walk away to Vinnie C's, blushing again. Ben yelled, "COUNT ON IT !" Ben saw Monica on the phone, standing by her car, and left.

Monica stood for a few minutes, checking the text messages, before going inside her car. Monica then called Renee back. Renee picked up, sitting at the living room couch, reading a catalog. Monica said, "Renee, hello?"

Renee, turning the pages, answered, "Hey Chi Chi ! What's up?" Monica, feeling joyful, said, "Hey. Well, aside from running into Bird and Linda at Vinnie C's. Do you remember that guy we saw hiking? Well. ….. When we were leaving?" Renee, thinking then remember, answering, "Wait ! That cutie in the green shirt, right?" Monica answered, "Guess what?" Renee, waiting on the answer, responded, "What's up?" Monica said, "He asked me out !" Renee dropped the catalog and got up from the couch with such excitement and asked, "How? Where? When? Details please !" Monica began to explain the details, saying, "Ok. So at Vinnie C's, he just so happened to be outside already. He forgot his item list; he then recognized me." Renee, thinking on what was said, said, "That's so random but continue, Chi Chi. He then recognizes you? …. Who is he?" Feng then came out of the bathroom and saw Renee on the phone, asking, "Who is it?" Renee, sitting back on the couch, answered, "It's Chi Chi." Monica then got inside the car, throwing her purse at the passenger seat, closing the door, and then starting the engine up and saying, "I'm headed home now. I will tell you more later." Monica then hung up and placed the phone at the passenger seat, then drove off, heading home. Monica began to have thoughts on what her father would say but was willing to take a chance with Carmen. She then approached a red light and stopped in thought of what if Carmen is the one.

Within a few minutes at the De Nino's residence, Renee heard a knock at the door. She got up from the couch and saw her father through the square glass on the door. Renee then opened and closed the door, kissing her father on the cheek and saying, "Hey Pop !" Sylvester, holding documents under his left arm, asked, "How's everyone doing?" Feng smiled and waved at him. Renee walked to the kitchen where Feng was. Sylvester walked into the living room and saw them open the refrigerator. Feng asked, "Sylvester, what's good?" Sylvester stood around the family portraits and answered, "I've been good. Ready to start something new, you know." Feng then sat a gallon of orange juice at the kitchen table, closing the refrigerator and answered, "I heard that." Sylvester looked around and noticed Monica wasn't present. He saw Renee reaching in a cabinet for two glasses. Sylvester then asked, "Where's Chi Chi?" Renee, using the gallon at the kitchen table and pouring the orange juice into the glasses for them, replied, "She's coming. I know you like your orange juice, Pop."

Renee walked over and handed Sylvester a glass of orange juice. He held the glass, looking at the pictures of Marie with the girls in the late nineties. Renee glanced at Sylvester after taking a sip of orange juice and said, "Monica said she had ran into Bird and Linda at Vinnie C's." Sylvester smirked at the comment and answered, "Bird. I haven't seen him in years; he had a thing for your mother, I tell ya. Yeah, Bird and I really don't get along, Renee." Renee, nodding her head, said, "Just thought you should know, Pop."

Feng walked out of the kitchen to where they were. He glanced at Sylvester, asking, "Hey. Are you staying for the basketball game tonight?" Sylvester answered, "Maybe next time. I bought my work with me. My mind is somewhere else." Renee looked at the documents and asked, "What's this, Pop?" Sylvester saw she was looking and answered, "It's the art gallery idea paperwork; it's all business." Renee gazed at her father with the thought of him being a busybody and said, "Dad, you're more than welcome to stay and have dinner with us, you know." Sylvester then finished the glass and handed it back to her. He saw a loaf of bread and a fruit basket on the kitchen table. Sylvester, being sarcastic, then mentioned, "Wait? There's food here?" Renee, knowing he was joking, began to chuckle at the comment and answered, "Yes sir. Surprise, surprise. Right?" Renee said again, "You're always welcome to stay and have dinner with us." Sylvester smiled and answered, "Thank you." Renee, with a question, then asked, "So, yesterday was your last day at work right?" Sylvester answered, "Yeah. I was headed over here but my boss wanted to have lunch with me." Renee said, "I understand."

Renee then walked away into the kitchen, with Feng putting the glasses in the sink. Sylvester then gazed at a picture of himself with Dean fishing together. Feng, watching

Sylvester look at the family portraits, asked, "Renee, does he always look at those pictures?" Renee reached for his hand and answered, "We are his heart. You should get to know him since we are together, the father-in-law thing, you know." Sylvester then got himself ready to leave and they all heard a knock at the door. Feng gazed at the door and said, "I bet that's Chi Chi !"

Chapter 4

When it Comes to Family !

Monica then opened the door with the three grocery bags on the ground. She saw Sylvester and got excited and said, "Pop? Hey ! I didn't know you were here. I saw a red sports car; is that you?" Sylvester then left his documents on the kitchen counter, walked over, and gave her a hand, reaching for two bags and headed to the kitchen table. Sylvester then sat the groceries down and answered, "Yeah, that's my weekend car. I would have open the door for ya, but you're too quick with the keys." Monica then locked the door and went into the kitchen with her purse and the last bag. She laid the bag on the table, then kissed Sylvester on the cheek. Sylvester reached for his documents, watching Feng and Renee go sit on the couch. Monica then sat her keys and purse down at the table, saying, "Feng normally helps me with the bags. Thanks Pop." Monica started putting the food away. She gazed over at the TV for a minute, asking, "What are you guys watching?" Renee and Feng didn't answer because the show caught their attention. Sylvester then looked around the kitchen and said, "Alright. I gotta go and look over these documents at home. I'll be in touch."

Monica, wanting to hear her father's thoughts, quickly said, "Hey Pop, I met someone !" Sylvester turned around and gave his full attention, answering, "Who? Today? Who's the lucky guy?" Renee, holding the remote, turned the volume down to hear their conversation. Feng then, disturbed that the volume was low, asked, "Renee, why?" Renee pointed at the kitchen and said, "Listen." Monica then answered, "You know the family, Pop." Sylvester waited for her to continue while figuring out who. She then went on to say, "It's Carmen Lagaipa. You know, Paul's son." When Monica answered back, Renee frowned and got up from the couch, upset. Feng still seated, saw Renee's expression, and then standing asked, "Renee? What's up?" Renee ignored Feng and glanced at Monica with an attitude says, "Why didn't you say it was Paul's son? This whole time I thought it was some other guy !" Monica heard her sister out and took notice that her father stared at her with such disappointment. Monica then said, "I thought all was forgiven?"

Sylvester took a breather and slowly asked, "When did this happen?" Monica replied, "Almost a half hour ago. Pop, you ok?" Feng then got up and stood next to Renee, knowing there was tension. He remained silent and continued listening. Sylvester looked away and asked, "What's his intentions with you?" Monica knew right then and there her father wouldn't approve of them talking so she, in a childish voice, pleaded and said, "Daddy?" Renee quickly intruded, saying, "Chi Chi, some other guy ! This is hard for Pop and me." Monica disagreed, answering, "This guy I like, Pop. It's just a date; If he isn't any good, then I won't continue with him." Feng gazed at Renee, asking, "Who's Carmen?" Renee answered, "Paul's son. The Paul I told you about, or not." Sylvester glanced at Monica, reaching for his keys, asked, "And you like this guy?" Monica being honest, with her arms cross and looking at everyone, answered, "Yes."

Sylvester then walked out of the kitchen to the door, turned around with all eyes on him. He arguably stated, "Monica, what do you want me to say to you? You want to date the son of the guy who killed your mother, and yeah, after a decade, I finally forgave Paul ! ….. Monica, how could you !" Renee then walked over to comfort Monica, looking down at the kitchen table and listening to their father. Sylvester then opened the door, looking at Monica heated, and said, "I can't do this; I don't know what else to say to you right now !" Sylvester then closed the door. Monica, upset with tears, mentioned, "If he forgave, then why doesn't he like me going out with this guy?" Monica then gazed at Renee, not saying a word, who give her a napkin from the counter. Monica asked, "Renee, you feel he is right?" She then wiped her tears, waiting on Renee's answer.

Renee then took a breather and answered, "Carmen's father killed Mom, you know this." Monica, still upset, yelled, "YEAH HIS FATHER DID, BUT CARMEN IS INNOCENT, RENEE! YOU CAN'T BLAME HIM! …. I AM SURE HE IS NOTHING LIKE HIS FATHER!" Renee, in a relaxing voice, responded, "All right, you test the waters out if ya want . … You and I see Pop come and look at the family portraits every time he visits . …. Monica ….How could you even consider dating him.?"Monica had tears streaming down her face again. She then walked away, yelling, "NOBODY CARES HOW I FEEL!" Monica went into her room and slammed the door closed. Feng then walked into the kitchen with Renee to comfort her with a hug.

Renee glanced at Feng and said, "I thought she'd under-stand her being the oldest. I didn't even get a chance to tell my father I met your folks." Feng answered, "Well, now is not a good time." Renee then asked, "Am I wrong or..?" Feng smiled and answered, "It's a bad idea for Chi Chi. I believe Sylvester is hurt based on her poor decision; you should call him." Renee agreed, then look at what was inside the bags on the kitchen table. Feng then leaned on the counter, looking at the bags and said, "I'll help you cook;

don't ask Chi Chi." Renee smiled and they kissed, starting lunch, which became dinner for the day together. Renee then reached into a bag and held a tomato sauce can, saying, "You're right. I'll give her space. In the meantime, I will start cooking the beef. You can pour the gravy though." Monica was in her room, laying on the bed, thinking about everything and felt misunderstood.

Sylvester finally arrived home later that afternoon. He stayed in the car deep in thought about Monica and realized she wasn't a child anymore. Sylvester glanced at the documents next to his phone on the passenger seat. He then came out of the car, receiving a phone call. Sylvester looked and saw it was Renee so he answered, "Yeah?" Renee, in the kitchen, watched Feng pour the gravy into a pot with beef and said, "Dad. I'm just checking on you. You ok?" Sylvester then closed the door, locking the car and walking to the front door of the house. He looked around and answered, "I will be. Help me understand because I don't get it. I'm just disappointed in your sister's decision is all. Why that family, you know?" Sylvester then opened and closed the door, turning the lights on in the living room and tossing the keys onto the table. Renee then sat down at the kitchen table and answered, "I'm going to talk to her again once she calms down for the family's sake. Alright, Pop?" Sylvester then sat at his chair around a widescreen TV and said, "Alright. Love you girls. Keep me posted." They both hung up and he was left with the thought being why him.

Sylvester then got up and went into his office. He looked at his laptop and turned it on. He left it on emails and had received a message from the realtor named La La in regards to a building. Sylvester then sat down and responded to the email; within eight minutes they then set up an appointment for the building.

Feng watched Renee leave her cell phone at the kitchen table and helped cook for a good twenty minutes. Feng, clueless to the conversation, asked, "So, what's up?" Renee then reached into a cabinet nearby for plates and answered, "It's like this. …. If she wants to go out with Carmen, I will help her get dressed up. After all, she is my sister and I want to make her happy. What a tough situation. Right?" Renee then turned the stove off and continued on to say, "Feng, she'd do it for me. Ready to eat?" Feng began to sit at the table, worried about Monica missing out on dinner and made a comment, "Should we call Monica for dinner or …?" Renee then made their plates full with food and sat at the kitchen table again. Putting her hair into a bun, she answered, "Let me deal with her." Feng agreed, then they ate supper. They made a combination of pasta, mushrooms, gravy and very little beef. Feng enjoyed dinner talking about how good the food was. Renee smiled and said, "Like my mother would said, 'You're Italian, do it right!'" They both laugh and continued eating.

That evening, as it began to get cloudy around 10:44 pm, Carmen, Ben, and Victor were at a diner gossiping about everything in downtown New Haven. While they waited for their food, Victor asked, "Carmen, question?" Carmen gave him his full attention. Then, after looking around, Victor went on to say, "When this thing is done, what are you gonna do with your money?" Carmen laughed at the remark and answered, "That's a good question." Carmen looked at the window, then back at Victor and said, "Leave the country and start a new life out in Europe. France maybe." The waiter then came over with the food and drinks., Putting the plates down on their table, he asked, "Is there anything else I can get for you?" They waved him off.

Victor gazed at Carmen and asked, "Hey boss ! What about the big man with them?" Carmen smirked at the comment and answered, "There is nothing a bullet can't solve. Keep in mind I will be meeting with two other guys." Victor, then eating a cheeseburger, looked around the diner again and, under his breath, said, "Sounds like an easy job, boss." Victor then went on to ask with sarcasm, "Boss, she really believes you both are going out on a date?" They all laughed at the comment. Carmen answered, "Yeah, I'm aiming for 6 pm." Ben, out of lusting after the girl's beauty, eating French fries and said, "Those girls are knockouts, boss !" Carmen smiled and took a sip of soda and said, "Tell me about it; this should be easy." While they were eating, Ben received a phone call from Lisa; the phone was near his drink at the table. Ben then sat his fries back on the plate. He held the phone up and saw the missed call was Lisa. Carmen asked, "Who was it?" Ben smiled and replied, "Some girl I met earlier. I don't have a picture of her yet."

Ben then got up and said, "I gotta take this call or I won't hear the end of it. Be right back." Ben then walked to the bathroom calling Lisa back. Victor looked at Carmen and asked, "Boss, you grew up with these people? I remember what you said about your father in regards to a partnership." Carmen nodding his head and answered, "I only been around the De Ninos twice in my life with my father. Back home, my father only spoke about the millions Sylvester told him about in his father's will. My father spoke about it so much that he promised me a better life. The neighborhood I grew up in and the way my father was with my mother and I was something else. My father needed help with his drinking habit." Victor understood and, with sarcasm, said, "I never knew my father."

Victor then raised his glass filled with soda to Carmen and softly uttered, "Here's to the money !" Carmen raised his glass in agreement with Victor and declared, "The money. No more waste management for me; if my father were alive to know what I am about to receive." Victor then sat down his glass with Carmen, reaching for French fries and replied, "You think her father will kill you?" Carmen sat back and gazed at Victor, answering, "Nope. His daughters are his heart. I am sure of this. If he is smart, he will give me what I want. I am not worried at all." While they were talking, Bird and his assistant manager named Angelo came inside the diner.

Victor saw them waiting at the entrance and got Carmen's attention. Carmen turned around and saw them. Carmen yelled, "HEY! BIRD, IS THAT YOU? …. BIRD LOMBARDI !" Angelo looked over and tapped Bird, asking, "Bird. You know those kids?" Bird glanced over as the waiter came to them, looking around for a seat for two. Bird waved at Carmen and answered, "Hey kid !" The diner didn't have a lot of people so the waiter seated them close to the entrance and said, "My name is Bruce. I will be with you both in a few minutes." After being seated, Angelo said, "This morning I had to let a few people go; they wouldn't step it up, Bird. And I know we need the help and all but the callouts you know, it gets us nowhere !"

Bird quickly answered, "Angelo, I am the owner; you know this. It looks bad when you step out of line like yelling at human resources for doing the job of two people. I think it was a mistake having you as my assistant manager because you're making this a habit. We don't abuse power; I don't need that kind of heat." Angelo, looking away, said, "All right. All right, I will prove to you that I can do better. Not for nothing but the other managers are way too laid back." Bird looked over at their waiter talking with the manager.

To the left he saw two waiters serving customers and said, "I asked you to join me tonight to make sure when you go to work tomorrow, you know your role." Angelo agreed and said, "All right boss; I'll zip it." Bird, not believing him, said, "Angelo, do what I tell you !" Bird then got up and asked a waiter close to them where the bathroom was and the waiter answered. Angelo watched Bird walk to the bathroom immediately.

Bird passed Carmen with Victor going to the restroom. Carmen said, "I'mma tell you right now; my father never liked that guy. Bird was against the partnership and wasn't fond of my father also !" Victor looked back and said, "Maybe we do him sometime, right?" Carmen smirked at what was said and, under his breath, mumbled, "All I want is those millions. Bird is a waste of time. We're not murderers." The waiter serving Bird with Angelo then came over to Angelo, asking, "Are you ready to order?" Angelo looked ahead for Bird, then quickly answered, "Give us a few minutes, will ya?" The waiter agreed and walked away.

Bird was in the bathroom using the urinal stool, hearing Ben on the phone. Ben was on the phone, looking down around the sink. He then looked over and recognizing it was Bird. Ben smiled, then looked into the mirror and said, "So, you know Carmen too? …. Where are you now? Lisa answered, "Carmen Lagiapa, a little. My father knew his father. …. I'm at a friend's house." Ben says,"Small world, isn't it?. Listen,

I'mma call you back. Alright? Bye." Ben then hung up and said, "Bird? Hey." Bird finished, then glanced at Ben and seeing they were the only ones in the bathroom, answered, "Hey kid." Ben, with a question, asked, "Question: Do you know a Lisa Lombardi? Green eyes with long, dark, curly hair?" Bird, making his way to the sink, stopped and stared at Ben, replying, "Yes I do. Why?" Before Ben could answer, Angelo came into the restroom and told Bird their waiter was waiting on them. Bird turned his attention back at Ben and questioned him why again. Ben answered, "I don't know too many Lombardi's."

Bird, being curious, asked, "Why you ask me; rather what are you asking me?" Ben became afraid and quickly answered, "This girl has a small heart tattoo on her neck. She of no relations to you. Right? We're talking and she might become my girlfriend. I'm just making sure, Bird." When Bird heard the mention of a heart tattoo, he knew then it was his daughter. Bird's face began to change to red and he yelled, "LOCK THE DOOR, ANGELO !" Bird then pushed Ben up against the wall and angrily yelled, "THAT'S MY DAUGHTER ! MY DAUGHTER, YOU HEAR ME !" Angelo then ran over and tries to get in between the two, saying, "Boss, keep claim !" Bird then took three steps away and thought of why Lisa didn't tell him about Ben. Angelo glanced at Bird and asked, "You ok, boss?" Ben stood against the wall, not knowing what to do, and commented, "Lisa should have told you ! …. I didn't know that was your daughter !" Bird figured it out, knowing she knew his answer on dating Ben would've been no. Bird then stepped to Ben again and punched him in the mouth, watching him fall to the floor bleeding. Bird looked at Ben, then in a demanding loud voice yelled, "I KNOW WHO YOU RUN WITH ! .. . .. YOU STAY AWAY FROM MY DAUGHTER! ... ANGELO, LET'S GO!"

Bird left with Angelo concerned for his daughter. Ben then got up, looking at the blood from his mouth in the mirror, turning the sink on with the thought of Lisa being in trouble. Carmen looked in the direction of the bathroom and mentioned Ben has been in there for a while. Ben quickly dusted himself off and called Lisa back. Lisa picked up, lying in bed, and answered, "That was quick. So where were we?" Ben reached for some tissue around the sink to wipe the blood from his mouth and said, "Listen, I don't know how to say this but...I can't talk to you anymore !" Lisa then frowned and got up from a bed, saying, "Wait. What? What happened?" Lisa stood, waiting for an answer but got none. She then said, "You're not gonna even tell me why, right? You know what, lose my number !" Lisa's friend Amanda, at the time, overheard her while walking in her room asked, "Lisa, what's wrong?" Ben finished wiping his mouth, frustrated, and balled the tissue up, throwing it at the mirror and yelling, "WE'RE DONE HERE !" Ben then hung up, turned the sink off, and then headed back to their table. Victor glanced at Ben walking over and taking a seat, and asked, "Bro, you ok in there?" Ben, wiping his mouth with his hand, answered, "Yeah . ... women."

Bird got on the phone driving with Angelo in his black SUV. Linda then received a phone call from Bird, lying in bed. Linda saw with her phone nearby and answered, "Yes, love?" Bird, looking around while driving, replied, "Hey. Is Lisa there?" Linda, wondering why, sat up and responded, "She's with her friend Amanda. Why? What's up?" Bird then stopped at a red stop light and questioned Linda, saying, "Linda, why didn't you tell me Lisa was talking to someone?" Angelo then zoned out of their conversation and looked away. Linda answered, "Bird, she's twenty-one years old. They just started talking today so nothing is really official." Bird saw the light turn green. He sped up and quickly responded, "But you knew about it, all right." Linda then realized this had bothered Bird, so she said, "Sorry. I am sure Lisa was gonna tell you once it was official." Bird approached another stop light on yellow, so he sped up, frustrated and hung up. Linda, worried, said, "Hello? Hello? Bird ! ... . I don't believe this." Angelo then asked, "Boss, is everything alright?" Bird heard but gave no answer, driving Angelo back home that evening.

Chapter 5

Let's Talk it Out !

eanwhile, the next day around 6:45 a.m. at Steve's apartment, he received a call in bed. Steve then got up and looked at the clock next to his phone on the bed dresser. When Steve saw the time, he then checked his phone and recognized the missed call was Samantha. Steve then thought to himself, *Why is Samantha calling me so early?* He then called back. Samantha picked up and said, "Morning Steve. Listen, don't come in today." Steve got curious and asked, "Why?" Samantha answered, "I need you and Bret tomorrow rather than today, ok?" Steve then scratched his head and replied, "Ok, see you tomorrow then."Steve then hung up and stayed in bed, smiling.

Samantha, sitting in her office with the door opened, yelled, "RITA ! …. RITA !" Rita heard Samantha's voice and stopped the conversation with the employees in the break-room, walking the halls with her clipboard to the office and answering, "Yes?" Samantha glanced at her and asked, "How many interviews today?" Rita replied, "I believe six. But one of them said he wouldn't be able to come today." Samantha asked, "How many already here?" Rita then glanced at the clipboard and answered, "You have three ready for their interview. You want me to get one of them now?" Samantha shook her head yes, looking at documents while waiting. Rita gave their resumes to Samantha and went into the waiting room and let a young lady dressed casually, Cathy, know she could come and get an interview. A guy named Terry and an middle aged lady named Grace watched and continued to wait for their turns.

Cathy followed Rita into the office and was invited to have a seat. She then sat down, watching Samantha sign some documents. Rita replied, "She will be right with you." Rita then closed the door and stood outside the office, waiting for the interview to be over. Cathy looked at the door, then immediately noticed the sweet mixture aroma from a bowl at Samantha's desk and said, "It smells really good in your office." Samantha then glanced at Cathy and smirked while reading her resume. Samantha then went over the resume, asking,"Cathy, thanks for being here early. Now please …. tell me about yourself." Cathy then gave her full attention and answered, "Well, I love to party. I have two dogs at home. I am from Greenwich. ... " Samantha then stopped her and inquired, "Do you have any computer skills? I see creative writing but do you have any computer skills?" They then laughed at the misunderstanding. Cathy then looked at what Samantha was wearing and complimented her, saying, "Wow ! I have that same blue dress. Did you get it from the mall?.. I'm sorry, you said skills. Right?" Samantha stared at her, knowing she gets way too distracted yelled, "RITA !"Rita then opened the door and stood by Cathy. Samantha smiled and said, "We'll be in touch, ok?" Cathy then got up from her seat, confused. Hoping to hear back, she then followed Rita out of the office. Rita stood and watched her exit the building said, "Have a good day. "Terry and Grace looked all around the area seated and saw in front of them Laura the secretary at her desk working. Across was Samantha's office, then the hallway in between.

Rita then got the okay for the next person. She went over to the waiting room for Terry and asked, "Terry, are you ready?" Terry then got up and followed Rita into the office and took a seat. He then watched the door close. Terry then watched Samantha hold and review his resume, asking, "Excuse me, two things. How long is this going to take? Also I can't work the weekends. I have a night job during the week." Samantha then sat the resume down and gazed at him, asking, "I don't see any computer skills on your resume, why?" Terry then looked at his watch and answered, "Don't you guys train here?" Samantha smiled at the comment made and yelled, "RITA !" Grace, at that time, immediately noticed that the two interviews before her were way too quick. She watched Rita walk the young man out. Terry with Rita, trying to figure out what happened, replied, "I don't understand we will call you." "You either train or don't. Right?" Terry walked out and Rita came to Grace, asking, "Miss, are you ready for your interview?"

Samantha then rested her head on the chair, being aggravated with the thought of does anybody wanna work. Rita, with Grace, went into the office and stood around the door. Samantha saw and waved them in, saying, "You're welcome to have a seat." Grace took a seat watching Rita leave and Samantha with her resume. Grace immediately noticed the sweet aroma in the room and the door left opened. Grace got worried then, so out of being curious, she asked, "Can I ask what you are looking for?" Samantha took a breather and answered, "I want someone that has computer skills and will come to work. Do you have computer skills?" Grace shook her head yes and replied, "I started doing graphics in the nineties. I went to a community college out in White Plains and graduated. I lived in New York for seventeen years, married with kids at the time. I now live here down the road."

Samantha, with a serious look, asked, "Why should I hire you?" Grace began to think on a good enough reason and answered, "I believe I will be a great help for Samantha's Way ! Whatever you need." Samantha liked the answer that was given. She then got up and walked to the window, asking, "Can you work weekends if needed?" Grace replied, "Not all but some. I also have a daughter named Tina that's good with computers; she is looking for work also." Samantha then turned around, facing her with a grin and said, "Oh really?" Rita then came in the office and said, "Your 7:45 am interview is early but here." Samantha then went back to her seat and looked over the resume again, saying, "Thank Rita." Samantha then got up and shook Grace's hand, saying, "You got the job !" Grace, excited, got up and said, "Thank you Miss Santino !" Samantha smiled and answered, "Samantha is fine. The number on your resume is the best contact number?" Grace replied, "Yes, it is !" Samantha smiled and sat back down, saying, "I will let you know when you'll start, ok?" Grace smiled and followed Rita out.

Rita shortly returned to Samantha's office to get a feeling on the people that had already been interviewed. Rita inquired, "Well, what do you think so far?" Samantha took a breather and answered, "I like Grace. When I call her, I will ask about her daughter also. How do I look by the way?" Rita glanced at her and replied, "You look fine, boss ! Glad you're interviewing everyone today because we need the help bad. Monica is coming back Monday so that's a plus. Hang in there, boss !" Samantha then put her hair in a ponytail and said, "All I want right now is the next

Monica De Nino, like six of them. Hardworking, on time, and dedicated. .... I am ready for the next person; you can bring whoever is here now." Rita then went to the waiting room for the next person.

That same morning at Bird's house, Bird and Linda sat eating breakfast at the kitchen table, dressed causal. Bird was looking at the newspapers, holding half a sausage, ready to chew; Linda then received a call from Lisa. Linda saw and reached for her phone near her plate and answered, "Morning. How was your girls' night?" Linda then received bad news from her daughter about Ben. She heard the disappointment but was trying to understand the situation. Linda looked away from Bird, saying, "Wait. What?" Bird turned his attention to hear but couldn't; he then waited for her to give a name while turning a page. Linda said, "You barely knew him. Yes, I'm saying?" Bird smiled, having an idea at the remark, and took a sip of black coffee. Linda said, "Listen, Lisa! .... I understand that but there are millions of men out there, sweetheart."

Linda then got up and walked into the living room, hearing Lisa vent out. Bird watched and sat the cup down. Lisa, at the time, was around the mirror in the bathroom, saying, "It's wrong to accuse Dad of scaring Ben off; he doesn't know we were talking. Right?" Linda then glanced back at Bird, holding and reviewing the newspapers lies, and answered, "He doesn't know. Question: Why is it a secret?"

Lisa, rolling her eyes at the comment, answered, "He hangs out with Carmen Lagaipa. Dad doesn't like that family because Paul driving drunk killed Marie and his godson." Linda remembered and said, "I get it, I see." Bird then put down the newspapers, got up, and started walking into the living room, passing Linda. Bird stopped at the door, waiting to question Linda. Linda then made eye contact with Bird, asking, "You wanna say something to your father before he heads out?" Lisa, coming out the bathroom, answered, "No." Linda looked at the floor and said, "Alright. Have a good day, sweetie." Lisa then hung up.

Bird mentioned, "The talking thing between Ben and Lisa, right?" Linda gazed at him and nodded yes. Linda then realized he was leaving asked, "Where are you headed?" Bird, reaching into his pocket for the keys, answered, "I got to go down to the office to get a few things; Angelo is waiting on me. I'll be right back. Question, what was the reason she didn't want me to know about this guy?" Linda then took a breather and answered, "Ben is friends with the Lagaipas was the reason. Lisa is a beautiful, young lady; a lot of guys are intimidated by her. She's been single for at least three years now." Bird, being disappointed, said, "This I don't like this ! Linda, I am glad it's over now !" Bird opened, then slammed the door closed. Linda had that same thought in mind.

Feng, around that time, was inside a gas station looking at snacks with very few people around. Feng's uncle, named Ken Feng, Lo Feng's older brother, came inside for gas and saw Feng. Ken Feng was tall, lean, and funny with short, dark gel hair. Ken walked over to him. They greeted with a handshake. Ken asked, "How's everyone? I ask your father about you." Feng, reaching for a bag of chips, replied, "Things are good with me." Ken, being curious, then asked, "So, how's your love life with Nia?" Feng laughed at the remark and answered, "We broke up some time ago; she is in New Jersey. Let me show you my new girlfriend." Feng then held a bag of chips, reaching into his back pocket to show Ken with his phone.

Ken glanced and smiled at a picture of Renee, saying, "Wow, blonde? She's beautiful; congratulations." While Feng and Ken talked, Feng's former coworker named Tylor from the club was outside pumping gas with his friends, Beckham and Andrew. Tylor looked inside and saw Feng and got upset. Andrew then took noticed and asked, "What's wrong?" Tylor glanced at Andrew and replied, "The big guy talking to the Asian guy inside cost me my job at the club. We were coworkers and I haven't had a break since." Tylor then looked at his friend, knowing they were on his side, lied and said, "He lied and told our boss I was allowing underage girls inside the club. He also attacked me for no reason at a shopping plaza in East Haven; the guy just doesn't like me!" Beckham and Andrew frowned at the remark. Andrew then pointed at Feng and asked, "The big guy putting back the chips, right?" Tylor nodded yes; they then waited for Feng to come out to get even.

Feng, at that time, was laughing at a comment Ken had made. He then had a question so he asked, "Ken, how come you don't visit your brother at church?" Ken then stood to the cashier and paid for gas, replying, "Since we were small, your father has been preaching to me. 'Repent ! Repent for the kingdom of God is at hand, ' he would say." They then laughed, coming outside. Tylor, Andrew, and Beckham stared at them, standing three feet away. Ken quickly asked, "What's this?" Andrew mean-mugged him and then stared at Feng, shouting, "HEY BIG GUY ! ... YOU ATTACK THIS GUY?" Ken then watched Andrew point at Tylor, looking at Feng. Ken asked, "Feng, who are these people?" Feng replied, "Tylor, a former coworker is the one in the middle. The other two seems to be friends, I guess." Andrew, feeling ignored, again shouted, "HEY, I AM TALKING TO YOU !"

Bret and Steve, around that time, made their way driving to the gas station in a truck. They then parked behind Feng's SUV for gas and saw the stare-down between the fellas. Beckham then got in Feng's face, saying, "Try me; I dare you !" Ken then pushed Beckham away from Feng, saying, "We don't want trouble so please leave us !" Beckham then sucker-punched Ken in the face. Tylor with Andrew attacked

Feng. Bret and Steve were stunned and didn't know what to do but watch.

The manager saw them fighting and ran outside, yelling, "HEY! …. I'LL CALL THE COPS! HEY, STOP FIGHTING!" Feng, in defense of being grabbed from behind, head-butted Andrew's nose. Andrew fell down, bleeding. Feng then turned around and blocked a punch from Tylor with his right arm, then kicked him in the groin. Tylor reacted to the blow, holding his groin area, and then was punched in the face by Feng, falling down. Andrew then got up angry and attacked Feng from behind again, using his height with his arms around his neck. Feng, in a violent manner, squeezed his groin area. After hearing Andrew yell in pain, his neck was released. Feng then turned around and punched Andrew in the face, watching him fall knockout. Feng then watched Ken give a round house kick to Beckham, leaving him knock out on the ground. Some customers amazed had their phones out recording the fight.

Feng glanced at the men knocked out on the ground. He then gazed at Ken, asking, "You ok?" Ken, taking a breather, looked around, replied, "Yeah! … Tell me later why they attack us. Let's go!" Feng watched Ken walk away, then mentioned, "Hey, you paid for gas!" Ken ignored the comment and drove away. Feng rushed inside his vehicle, leaving the gas station shortly after. Tylor and his friends got up within three minutes from being knocked out and saw customers with their phones recording them. Tylor got angry and yelled, "GET THOSE PHONES OUT OF MY FACE! … STOP RECORDING!" The manager and customers laughed at them and thought it was funny. Andrew and Beckham were embarrassed covering their faces. Bret and Steve were recording as well.

Sylvester, an hour later, waited for the realtor parked in front of the building alone, inside a plaza in East Haven. The meeting was to look inside the new commercial retail office building with a lot of space. The realtor La La then arrived and parked next to Sylvester. Sylvester then got out of the car and greeted La La with a handshake. La La, holding keys, then asked, "Are you ready, Mr. De Nino?" Sylvester then followed La La to the door, nodding yes. She opening the door and mentioned, "You are the first one to check out this building out. I remember what you wrote in the email. You had wanted to do this years ago, right?" Sylvester stood near the door, looking around, said, "Yes, I did." La La then glanced at his fingers and didn't see a married ring, asked, "So, you're running the business or your wife?"

Sylvester then stared at this corporately dressed brunette, wondering why she had asked that question. Sylvester then came inside and answered, "I will. By the way, do you normally work late?" La La, trying to understand him, replied, "You mean the emailing, right? I did that from home." Sylvester thought about her question, looking away said,

"I lost my wife and son." La La then realized she had asked the wrong question and said, "I apologize; I had no idea, sir ! I am so sorry. My condolences." Sylvester, looking around, said, "It's all right." Sylvester then walked around half of the building with La La. He noticed there was a huge amount of space inside the building. La La, being curious, then asked, "Do you paint?" Sylvester laughed at the comment and answered, "I don't paint but my daughters do." La La wanting to know more about his daughters, so she asked, "How many daughters do you have?" Sylvester then walked into an empty room, liking the space, and replied, "Two. How about yourself?" La La then stood and looked at the parking space through the window Sylvester was near answered, "I can't have kids; my husband and I tried." Sylvester looked at her out of concern and said, "Now I am feeling bad for asking you that question." La La looked down, smiled, and said, "It's fine. This is the printing room by the way."

La La then asked, "Are your daughters working with you?" Sylvester nodded yes, coming out of the printing room, and replied, "Yes. The commercial art gallery is finally happening." La La smiled at the comment and said, "Congratulations ! Let me show you the other side of the building before we leave. You have a huge amount of space for your projects. There are two offices in the back, our main hall, a conference room, restrooms, and a printing room. Follow me." Sylvester glanced around, liking the space, stopped and asked, "How much is the building?" La La answered, "1.2 million. I have everything in my car. I'm willing to work with you, sir."

Sylvester smiled at the comment and followed her, talking about the building. He then stopped and began to think about his family looking around. La La then took notice that he stopped following and kept quiet. She then waved her hand, trying to get his attention, saying, "Mr. De Nino? Mr. De Nino?" Sylvester then looked at her and answered, "Sorry, my head was somewhere else." La La laughed at the comment and asked, "How does five hundred thousand sound? Sylvester, surprised, asked, "Where do I sign?" La La and Sylvester spent an hour going over everything that afternoon.

Carmen, early that afternoon, was in a conversation with the secretary named Sally in his office. Sally was attractive and thin with long, blonde hair. Sally stop talking and looked at Carmen deep in thought, sitting at his desk. She then walked over to him, putting her hand on his shoulder. Carmen then turned his chair to Sally's direction and glanced at her. Sally started to rub his shoulder, then, in a bratty manner, asked, "Am I going to see you tonight?" Carmen smiled and replied, "No. Not tonight love. Something I gotta do." Sally then removed her hand and gave Carmen her full attention, asking, "So, when am I gonna see you?" Carmen then got up from his chair, smiling, and they kissed. After lusting at her, he said, "Tomorrow night should be fine." Carmen then walked over to the big office window with the blinds open, in thought of the church down the road. Carmen and his mother had visited that church at least twice in his life.

Sally stood around his chair. Watching him, she then looked down and saw a backpack close to the desk Sally thought nothing of the backpack and asked, "So, for tomorrow, can I leave early? I want to look good for you." Carmen then looked back at her again in a lustful manner and replied, "Yeah. You always look good, which is why we get into a lot of trouble here." Sally chuckled at the comment and, walking to the door, said, "Carmen?" Carmen, looking back answered, "Yeah." Sally questioned him, asking, "Instead of fooling around at work, do you think we could be lovers like in a relationship?" Carmen shook his head no and replied, "I'm in a different place in my life, and you have a boyfriend, so let's be real." Sally, feeling down about the remark, then opened and closed the door. Carmen then looked again at the window for a few minutes, then heard a knock at the door. Carmen then turned from the window and said, "Come in."

Chapter 6

The De'Ninos and Lagaipa's Don't Mix

en, with Victor, opened the door and came in the office, laughing at a joke said earlier in the breakroom. Ben looked at Carmen and said, "Hey boss? What's-her-name was looking for you earlier. Sally, right?" Ben watched Victory shrugged at the comment and then continued on to say, "I told Sally you were still here somewhere." Carmen answered, "I already spoke with her. Is everything set for tonight? Did you check the meeting grounds?" Victor answered, "Yes. Nobody hangs around those vacant buildings two blocks up." Ben then saw the backpack on the ground close to the desk and got curious, so he asked, "Boss, you have a backpack?" Carmen glanced at the backpack and replied, "I have two guns in there just in case . ... I can't take any chances with anything going wrong . .... I'm about to call these two guys." Victor asked, "Your date is still at 6pm, right?" Carmen then walked over to his desk and took a seat, answering, "Yeah, six is when my plan starts." Ben asked, "Do you think their father will get the cops involved, boss?" Carmen chuckled at the remark and answered, "If he is a smart man, he'd give me what I want privately. We get his daughters, then he will bend." Carmen then got up from his seat, putting the backpack on top of the desk saying, "Five million dollars . .... Ben, ever used a gun before?" Ben got excited and replied, "Yes, I have. I used to go out hunting with my father." Carmen then opened the backpack and handed Ben a gun and glanced at Victor, saying, "You only need to be a wheel man. You follow us there with the company van. I will give you a signal if her sister is in the house. Bret and Steve will help you out." Carmen then reached for a gun from the top desk drawer and pointed it at the door. Victor stood next to Carmen, asking, "Boss, who showed you how to uses a gun?" Carmen then put the gun back into the desk drawer and answered, "My mother; she always kept a piece because of the neighborhood." Ben, amazed with the gun check and saw it was loaded, asked, "Hey boss, where did you get the guns from?" Carmen laughed at the remark and replied, "Just know I know people. You seem happy. Victor, is he happy?" Victor watched Ben stare at the gun with a grin and replied, "He's happy, boss."

Carmen looked at his watch and saw it was 3:40 pm. Carmen said, "I gotta call this girl to let her know the date is at 6pm. After I close today, my two friends will meet us behind this building so we can gets started." Victor, smiling at the idea of having money, said, "Boss, we're the only ones here. The other employees left a hour ago. You know I never been to Italy before !" Ben laughed at the remark and replied, "Yeah? You know I would like to take a crack at Sally. Isn't she something !" Victor interrupted and made his point, saying, "I'm talking about when I get my share, Ben. Forget the women in this country. The women out of the country with this money, bro; I can get four Sally's, just saying." Carmen, hearing Sally's name, glanced at Ben and said, "Ben, you keep your hands off of Sally! …. She's mine." Ben, not knowing, quickly said, "I had no idea, boss; she's all yours !"

Monica, that same hour, was at her favorite coffee shop. She stood in front, looking at the menu, wearing dark shades, holding her purse. There were few people in line behind her, an employee saw her and, remembered a guy asking, told the manager. The manager then came over and asked, "What can I get for you?" Monica, not knowing what she wanted, replied, "I'll have my usual. One iced coffee, French vanilla cream with two sugars." The manager said, "Ok. Listen, some guy came in here asking for you, maybe a friend or your coworker. I don't know." Monica then removed her shades and asked, "Was his name Carmen, about 5'9", blue eyes with bleach blond hair and skinny?"

The manager laughed at the comment and answered, "Nobody like that. He said his name was Mitch. He was short, bald with a beard." Monica shook her head no looking at the swipe machine, reached into the purse for her credit card. Monica found it and swiped it on the machine, saying, "I don't know him; maybe he's a neighbor." The manager then made and finished her iced coffee, saying, "Well, have a good afternoon. Hopeful, I see you tomorrow?" Monica, putting her shades back on and receiving the iced coffee, answered, "Yeah, tomorrow." Monica's phone started to vibrate in her purse. Walking out, she checked and saw it was Carmen. Monica, excited, stood at the entrance and called back, saying, "Hey ! How's your day?" Carmen, out-side behind the building, replied, "Things are fine. How about yourself?"

Monica then walked to her car, holding the iced coffee, and saying, "Hearing your voice made my day. So, what time should we meet?" Carmen looked at his watch and answered, "Six. I forgot to tell you about that smile of yours. We can do whatever you want tonight. Question:, …. Do you have a sister? I have a friend that asked me . …. And I told him about you." Monica laughed at what was said and replied, "Yes, I have a sister. She has a boyfriend. My smile?" Carmen laughed at the remark and said, "The way you smile,

Monica, I gotta tell ya, I can't wait to see it again …. We both know about the past with our families but there is nothing love and forgiveness can't fix. Right? …. Am I right?" Monica got emotional and took a breather in shock of the comment. She felt like he understood her feelings. Monica then answered, "OH MY GOD, Carmen ! You so understand me !" Carmen said," I do . …. Well, I will see you at 6 pm." Monica answered, "Can't wait. Bye." Monica then hung up and went home to change for the date.

Feng with Renee, that same hour, were at a restaurant finishing their lunch. Renee, not in the best of moods, was concerned for Monica's blinded decision. Renee's phone near her glass received a text message. She seen it was from Monica in regards to the date. Feng, then using a napkin from the table to wipe his mouth, asked, "Thinking about Chi Chi again?" Renee looked at Feng and, with a very low voice, answered, "At the end of the day, she is still my sister. I just received a text from her saying her date is at 6 pm." Feng stated, "Where is she now?" Renee then reached for her purse at the table and got up from the seat, answering, "Home most likely. What time is it now?" Feng looked at his watch and replied, "It's 4:05. Are you ready to leave?" Renee nodded yes and said, "I'mma help her get ready for the date." Feng then waved at their waiter for the bill. The waiter saw and came over, giving the bill.

Feng paid the bill in cash, then left with Renee driving home. Renee reached for Feng's hand for comfort, looking at the window with her mind on the family. Feng then glanced at Renee, removing her hand and finding a song she would like on the radio. Renee stopped him, placing her hand back with his again. Feng then said, "Monica won't forget you helping her get ready for the date. She already knows how the family feels about it." Renee smiled at what was said and replied, "Keep this between us; something about this doesn't feel right, love." Feng, making a left turn into their street, answered, "Tell me about it."

Feng continued on and said, "Best thing we can do is be there for Monica, right?" They then entered the driveway and saw Monica's car park inside the garage with the garage door opened. Feng then parked behind her and turned the engine off. Feng glanced at Renee and, out of concern, said, "Renee, cheer up." Renee, frustrated with the situation, said, "What if he breaks her heart?" Feng then took a deep breath, looking straight ahead, and replied, "Well, he would be doing you a favor. Right?" Renee, not liking the comment, frowned and said, "I don't like that comment, Feng!" Feng then reminded Renee, saying, "You just said this doesn't feel right!" Renee, still frowning, opened her door, getting out of the SUV, and replied, "I know what I said. Let's just drop it! Ok?" Renee then closed her door, waiting for Feng to get out of the SUV.

Monica, at the time, was in her room, trying on different pairs of earrings in front of the mirror. She heard the door open and wondered who it was. Feng then closed the door, with Renee looking around shouting, "MONICA ! MONICA, WHERE ARE YOU?" Monica heard Renee and answered, "I'm in my room. Why?" Feng then went into the kitchen while Renee walked to her sister's door. Renee then stood at the door opened and watched Monica put down earrings. Monica glanced at Renee and asked, "What is it?" Renee then saw ten pairs of earrings on the dresser. She then helped Monica pick out the right earrings. Monica, not knowing Renee's motives, said, "I'm still going out with Carmen." Renee smiled at the comment and replied, "And that's why I am helping you, dear sister."

Monica got excited and hugged Renee. Monica then said, "Thank you so much ! I still don't know what to wear." Renee, in thought of Carmen, asked, "Did he call you today?" Monica then looked back at the mirror and answered, "When I left the coffee shop, he did . .... Renee, Carmen understands me. .... Even Pop spoke of forgiveness, remember?" Renee, listening, walked over to the opened closet and saw many summer dresses hanging. Renee then reached for two dresses, one peach and the other pale purple, and placed them on the bed. The house phone at the kitchen counter began to ring. Renee yelled to Feng to answer it. Feng was looking into the refrigerator for some juice to drink. He stopped and checked the house phone, recognizing it was Sylvester's number so he answered.

Feng, looking back into the refrigerator, on the phone said, "Hey Sylvester." Sylvester, at the time, stood in his front yard, looking around the neighborhood, and answered, "Feng, what's happening?" Feng, not wanting any soda, then closed the refrigerator and replied, "Things are good with Renee and I. We went out for lunch today and the food was really good. I gotta ask Renee what was the name of that restaurant again." Sylvester started to walk around the yard and asked, "Listen, I don't mean to be too forward but is Monica still talking or dating Paul's son?" Feng then peeped into the hall, hearing the ladies in the room talk about Carmen., He then went back into the kitchen and softly answered, "Yeah. Her mind is made up about this guy. Aren't you glad she didn't hide this from you?" Sylvester then walked to his car, worried and looking around the area, saying, "I am. I'd much rather her not do this. Question: Am I wrong for feeling this way?" Feng quickly answered, "Not at all." Sylvester then said, "Tell them I am down for dinner whenever." Feng then saw crumbs on top of the kitchen table. He wiped it with his hand, answering, "I'll let them know." Sylvester then hung up.

Feng hung up and put the phone back. He then went and stood at Monica's door, saying, "Your father said to let him know about dinner sometime." Monica gazed at Feng, confused and asking, "Pop said that?" Feng then looked at the dresses on her bed and replied, "Yes, he did. …. Renee, where did you put the remote?" Renee, looking at the dresses, asked, "How do you know I misplace the remote?" Feng then glanced at Renee and said, "Because I fell asleep and you were still watching that thriller movie like two in the morning." Renee answered, "Good point. Give me a minute. I am trying to pick out the right dress for her." Monica then raised up a pair of blue earrings. She glanced at Feng, waiting at the door while trying them on. Monica looked at herself with the earrings on in the mirror said, "The remote is near the kitchen sink. I was in the living room watching a sitcom earlier before I went out."

Feng, surprised, said, "Thanks." Feng then went back to the kitchen for the remote. Monica continued to think on what her father said and asked, "Why do you think Dad wants to have dinner with us?" Renee, still looking for the right dress in the closet, answered, "He wants to know about this kid you're talking to, love. Think about it; Pop did it with Feng and I, remember?" Monica then took off the blue earrings and reached for hoop earrings. Monica looked at the mirror, then turned around and glanced at the peach dress on the bed. Renee saw the hoop earrings, frowned and said, "No hoop earrings, Chi Chi !" Monica looked again at the mirror and agreed with the remark, saying, "Small earrings will work for tonight."

Monica then turned around, seeing Renee pick out a white, summer dress, laying it on the bed near a guitar. Renee asked, "Monica, what do you think?" Renee glanced at Monica, holding the small earrings and fidgeting. She knew Monica had a question, so she asked, "What's on your mind, Chi Chi?" Monica smiled and answered, "What if Carmen and Pop have dinner together, right? ...." Renee then distracted her by holding up the white dress for an approval. Monica nodded yes, watching her lay the dress on the bed. Renee then said, "Ok. So, I have to do your makeup and hair, even though your hairstyle is to your neck. Ever thought of growing your hair long again?" Renee then stood behind Monica, shaking her head no. She then looked for a brush and continued on to say, "If things are good with you guys, Pop is going to want to meet him. See what happens. Right?" Monica smiled at the comment made. Renee then saw the brush near the earrings and began to do her hair.

Shortly after the phone call, Sylvester held a glass of orange juice in his hand. He stood in the living room of his house, gazing at a family portrait on the wall. He took a sip, looking at Monica held by her mother. Sylvester then thought back on the argument before the accident between himself and Paul. Sylvester, disappointed, hoped his daughter had a change of heart.

Around 5:45 pm, Bret with Steve arrived at the waste management building on Webster Avenue. Victor was outside around the company van and saw them park. He then went into the office and told Carmen they're here. Carmen sat at his desk and grinned, then got up and said, "Tell them to come inside." Victor then went and told Bret and Steve to follow him inside to the office. Carmen was on the phone when they met. Carmen then glanced at Bret with Steve, saying, "Monica, I am on my way. Alright?" Monica, being excited, replied, "Can't wait. See ya soon." Bret and Steve looked around the office, then Ben came from behind and stood at the door, waiting for Carmen.

Bret glanced at Carmen, hanging up, asked, "What's up, these your peeps?" Carmen smiled at the remark, placing his phone on top of the desk, saying, "How you guys been?" Bret, being curious, said, "We're good, man ! Who are these men?" Carmen then walked up to them. Victor and Ben stared, waiting on their responses. Carmen came forward, saying, "Well, I trust you guys. So here it is, I need your help. We are going to kidnap a woman or two. I know these people and they comes from a family of money. Monica is the one I am talking with and this should be easy. The money will be more than enough. My question is, are you two in?" Carmen then walked over to his desk, reaching inside the top drawer. He then threw the younger photo and pointed Monica out on the desk. Carmen said, "We recently took pictures of Monica and her sister at a park."

Bret and Steve glanced at the picture and knew it was their co-worker. To protect Monica, they never mention knowing her. Bret frowned and asked, "Kidnapping? Why did you invite us to this? The answer is no !" Steve then shook his head no in agreement, frowning at Carmen. Ben then laughed at the comment, reaching for his gun from behind his waist. Steve began to worry and said, "You can't be serious, Carmen ! I know, growing up the three of us uses to steal candy bars and such but this !" Carmen remained focused says, "I am dead serious! …. Before my father had passed, he told me about the ten million in that family. So, we kidnap Monica and her sister if present for ransom with no worries. … Monica and I have a date tonight, and that is the plan, fellas." Carmen went on to reiterate, asking, "So, I ask you both again. This is the meat of the whole plan !"

Bret glared at the remark and said, "The meat of the whole plan? I believe we gave you an answer !" Ben now had them at gunpoint from behind. Carmen, disappointed in their answer, said, "Yes. I also have a plan of escape; ghosting if you may. I don't think you two have a choice now !" They both turned around and saw they were at gunpoint from behind. They then focused back at Carmen. Bret yelled, "I DON'T BELIEVE THIS ! LISTEN, WE AIN'T KIDNAPPING ANYONE !" Steve, agreeing with Bret watched Victor, stand next to Carmen. Ben said, "I had a funny feeling about these two, Carmen !" Carmen said, "Well, I guess we have a problem then !" Steve quickly attacked Ben by reaching for his arm to relieve the gun. Carmen saw Bret make a run, so he jumped and grabbed his legs, making him fall down. Victor gave Ben a hand, trying to hold Steve from behind. Steve then pushed Ben against the desk. Carmen then saw the photo fall from his desk, trying to keep a hold on Bret and yelling, "PUT THEM IN MY TRUNK !" Ben looked back at Carmen, asking, "Boss?" Carmen again yelled, "THESE TWO, IN MY TRUNK !"

Steve then caught Ben off guard, punching him in the face leaving him falling backwards, relieving the gun. The gun then fell and fired off at the big office window, leaving broken glass everywhere with the blinds opened. Two cops down the road on duty, due to a threat issue between two people over a parking space, heard the gun go off. One cop radioed it in, then came to investigate with his partner. When the cops got to the building, running on foot, a crowd of people around the area pointed to the building. The cops then rushed inside, armed, while the doors were still open into the hallway to Carmen's office. The officers then heard voices in his office, gave each other a signal, and then went into the office. The officers then saw a gun near the door; Victor and Ben holding Steve down to the ground; Carmen standing over Bret, having a gun pointed to his head and down on the ground. Carmen, making eye contact with Bret and not seeing the cops, said, "You lose, Bret !" Carmen then heard an officer from behind him yell, "FREEZE, DROP THE GUN NOW !" Carmen then dropped the gun, looking at the photo of Monica on the ground disappointed. Two cop cars arrived outside the building within five minutes. The arrests then were made.

Later in the afternoon, at the De Nino's home, Monica, wearing the white summer dress with accessories and a sweet perfume scent, waited for an hour at the front porch. Monica felt stood up, not hearing from Carmen. Renee with Feng were playing a lip-singing game in the living room. Renee stopped and glanced at the door being left opened and said, "I'll be right back." Feng, holding a little microphone, stopped and watched her walk outside replied, "Monica should have already left, right?" Renee outside saw Monica beautifully dress but her face had such disappointment. Renee said, "Chi Chi, it's been an hour. How about you join me and Feng inside? If Carmen stood you up, he doesn't deserve you." Monica, hearing her out, said, "He called me earlier. Maybe he will be late; I don't understand." Renee replied, "I know he did. Like you said, he could be late. Like, look at you in this dress. Mom would've said 'Know your ride home' . … In other words, check in with Jesus.'" Renee made Monica smile and hugged her out of comfort, then they came inside the house.

Within ten minutes, everyone heard a knock at the door. Monica, being eager that it might be Carmen, came to the door and asked, "Who is it?" A police officer says, "It the police ! … Can we have a minute of your time?" Feng heard, then turned the game off and met with Monica and Renee at the door. Monica then opened the door and saw two officers. She then wondered what they wanted. Monica then asked, "Can I help you two officers?" Officer Long introduced himself, along with his partner, Officer Banks. The police then showed their badges, standing at the door and focusing on everyone. Officer Long asked, "Are you or is there a Monica De Nino here?" Monica, being curious, answered, "I am Monica De Nino, why?" Officer Long then asked, "Can we have a word with you in private?"

Monica replied, "You can talk to me in front of them. What's up?" Officer Banks then handed her the photo from Carmen's office. She held the photo, wondering how they got it. Renee got curious, watching Monica from behind and asking, "Monica, what's going on?" Monica asked, "Who gave you this photo?" Monica handed the photo back to the officer, then looked at Renee in concern for their family.

Officer Long replied, "I take it that you haven't seen the news, right? …. Earlier over at Webster Avenue, there was an incident that almost involved a murder. We have two witnesses testifying against Carmen Lagaipa; one almost had gotten killed. The photo handed to you was at the scene. Officer Banks and I were the cops there." Renee, stunned in thought over the comment, said, "Carmen?" Monica, in a confused state, said, "That's crazy ! I don't believe this. Why?" The two officers continued staring at the three of them. Renee and Feng stared back in concern for Monica. Banks then noticed the disappointment on Monica's face and asked, "Who is Carmen Lagaipa to you?" Monica answered, "Just a guy who briefly knew my family and recently ask me out." Officer Long gazed at Monica and said, "That explains the recent phone calls. Bret Bevans and a Steve LaBranche said they knew you from work. Did you give Carmen your address?" Monica, surprised, covered her mouth with her hand and hearing those two names nodded yes. She then removed her hand, worried, and said, "Yes, Carmen knows my address. Bret and Steve are my coworkers; are they alright?" Renee then walked away, saying, "I'm calling Pop." Feng then walked up to the officers, asking, "Officers, is everything alright?" Officer Banks replied, "We are gonna have to take Monica in for more questioning if that's alright with you?" Officer Long frowned at the remark made by his partner; he felt they had their answer already. Monica then walked to the living room couch where her purse was, saying, "Oh, here we go."

Renee was in the hallway on the speaker phone with Sylvester. Out of concern, she began to pace back and forth, looking at the cops. Renee said, "The cops are here, Dad . .... Yeah . .... They are already here !" Sylvester, at the time, was sitting at the kitchen table. He got up in shock, not understanding why. Sylvester then asked, "Wait ! What's going on over there? Hello?" Renee then took a peep at the police, then turned around and said, "It's because of that

Carmen guy! Dad, where are you right now?" Sylvester then balled his fist, worried for Monica, says, "You gotta give me more! ….Is Feng there with ya? Did Carmen hit Monica?" Renee then walked over to the door and only saw Feng, asking, "Where's Monica?"

Feng glanced at Renee, asking, "Do you want to take a ride down to the police station with me, because they took her for questioning." They suddenly heard the doorknob move and opened and saw Monica. Feng then stared at Monica closing the door, confused that she never left. Renee walked over and hugged her, asking, "What happened? They didn't take you to the police station?" Monica replied, "I change my mind and decline on going with the police. Bret and Steve weren't involved in any criminal activity. They told me it was all about the millions we received. Officer Long told his partner that I had answered in regard to being questioned and that was good enough. ….Then I was told that the hearing is scheduled Monday at 10 am They gave me the address and also said it looks like it will go to trial. The trial they guess will most likely be two Mondays from now. I agreed to testify."

They all then heard Sylvester still on the speakerphone. Sylvester yelled, "HELLO?" Renee forgot, then answered, "Pop, Monica is here with us. Carmen was after the money!" Sylvester got upset with the comment made. He then calmed down and said, "Let me speak to Monica !" Renee then handed her phone over to Monica and watched. Monica then took a deep breath and glanced at Renee, not knowing what her father's reaction would be. Monica then threw her purse back on the couch and slowly replied, "Pop?" Sylvester said, "What are the cops doing about this kid? Are you ok?" After hearing his voice in a calm manner, Monica answered, "I'm ok. Carmen got arrested and has two guys testifying against him." Sylvester then felt at ease and said, "Well, more importantly, I am glad you all are safe."

Monica then walked into the kitchen and said, "Pop, I just want to apologize for putting you and Renee through this, you know. I couldn't get over this guy. I'm sorry, Pop." Sylvester replied, "Need I say it. The De Ninos and Lagaipas don't mix. I already told you the stove was hot, Monica !" Monica leaned up against the wall and said, "I understand where you're coming from, Pop." Feng stood in the living room with Renee, saying, "She won't ever forget that you were with her in this blinded decision." Renee smiled at the remark and said, "I wonder what or who stop this from happening." Feng shrugged his shoulders and answered, "Jesus, I believe ! You know He saves, love." Renee continued to watch Monica on the phone; she then thought on the comment that was made. Shortly after Monica and Sylvester spoke, she called around for a lawyer and got one by the name of Casey Logan. After Casey agreed to take the case, Monica then called Steve and Bret in regards to using her lawyer.

Chapter 7

The Key to the Future

The next day, on a sunny Saturday morning at the De Ninos home, Sylvester showed up to have breakfast with his daughters and a friend named Mario who was a chef. Sylvester knocked at the door with a bag of groceries under his left arm, waiting. He looked at Mario and said, "I don't know if they bought food or what?" Mario, with a puzzled expression, said, "What do you mean? Aren't your daughters Italian?" "Healthy foods can be the key to one's heart.. right?" Sylvester laughed at the comment, answering, "They are, and yes, key to one's heart ! What do you want me to tell ya?" Feng then opened the door and replied, "Welcome to my crib, you guys !" Mario was about to question who Feng was, until Sylvester said, "That's Feng. He's Renee's boyfriend." Mario then nodded.

They then came inside and went to the kitchen. Sylvester then sat down the bag on the kitchen table. Mario began to prepare the breakfast, taking the food out of the bag. Feng came into the kitchen, then glanced at Mario, asking, "Who are you, sir?" Sylvester smiled and answered, "This is Mario, my friend and chef. He cooked for me twice a week." Feng then walked into the living room and sat on the coach, saying, "Must be nice to have your own chef." Renee then came out of her room, wearing pink pajamas with slippers and putting her hair in a bun, heard the fellas talk. She then went to Sylvester, kissing him on the cheek. Renee, not expecting to see her father, said, "Pop, what's up?" Sylvester then came into the living room with Feng and replied, "I know I said dinner but I thought it'd be nice to start the day off with you all." Renee smiled and said, "That is so sweet of you, Pop."

Renee then glanced at Mario in the kitchen, not knowing who he was. Sylvester saw her reaction and answered, "That's Mario. He cooks for me here and there." Renee said, "Pop, next time check the refrigerator because there is food here. What's he making anyhow?" Mario, around the stove, organizing the breakfast, gazed at Renee and answered, "I make it all today. Eggs, sausage and bacon it all." Renee looked at her father and said, "You better watch your cholesterol, just saying." Sylvester avoided answering the remark and took notice of Monica's absents asked, "Where's your sister?" Renee began to chuckle and responded, "Pop, it's Saturday. She's in her room ! Good luck trying to get her up early."

Mario then began to cook and the smell of fresh food was all over the house. Sylvester, Feng, and Renee were in the living room in conversation of the situation that had happened last night. Monica, lying in bed, woke up smelling the food. She then heard her father's voice in the living room. Sylvester stood around the widescreen TV. Feng and Renee were sitting on the couch, listening. Sylvester asked, "Does she know what day the trial would be?" Feng answered, "I believe in two weeks. Ask Monica though." Renee nodded with her arms crossed.

Monica, wearing a white bathrobe and slippers, came out of her room standing in the hallway listening replied, "It's two Mondays from now, Pop, but who knows. Gotta go to the hearing first, right?" Sylvester watched her come into the living room. They kissed each other on the cheek. Monica then yawned, covering her month and surprised to see her father. Sylvester asked, "Did you rest well?" Monica glanced at Mario cooking in the kitchen and answered, "I did. …. Who is that in the kitchen cooking?" Renee reached over and joined Feng's hand, answering, "That is Pop's chef." They all stared at Sylvester. Sylvester annoyedly says, "He cooks like your mother alright ! …. So give me a break ! I'm no cook !" Sylvester then looked at Mario cooking asked, "Yo, Mario, how long?" Mario glanced at Sylvester and replied, "Twenty minutes I finish." Monica, in thought of court, looked at her father asked, "Pop, will you be there for me in court?" Sylvester smiled and answered, "Count on it. Your lawyer called me this morning in regards to my father's will. He said it would help your case. I take it you called him shortly after I was called last night."

Monica nodded yes, looking at Renee and saying, "Pop was right; the De Ninos and Lagaipas don't mix. You know it's been a year since I met someone; I am glad nothing happened." Sylvester, becoming curious, asked, "Your co-workers stopped the kidnapping was what the cops told you last night?" Monica nodded yes and answered, "Had it not been for Bret and Steve, you know." Feng focused on Monica and asked, "What was the connection with your co-workers and Carmen?" Monica shrugged her shoulders and answered, "In court, all will be revealed, right? If they stop the processes, then need I say more? Maybe they grew up together, who knows." Sylvester then waved his hand and got everyone's attention, saying, "Listen, after breakfast I want to show you guys the building for the art gallery. This is that Monday meeting we spoke about." Everyone became excited over the good news. Within fifteen minutes, they all ate breakfast at the kitchen table together.

That same morning at Samantha's Way, Samantha had arrived late in the parking lot. She parked and forgot her purse in a rush. Samantha had on dark shades coming inside the building, not really ready to do interviews again. Samantha met with Rita waiting at the entrance. She then removed her shades and asked, "Rita, did Bret or Steve show up today?" Rita nodded yes and said, "They are in the copy-and-print room, and Monica comes back Monday. Bret told me that he, Steve, and Monica have to go to a hearing in court. Bret didn't go into details with me." Samantha got curious and told Rita to have them come to her office. Samantha then went into her office frustrated, due to the lack of employees pacing back and forth. Rita then met with the fellas outside the copy-and-print room, conversing and said, "The boss wants to see you guys."

Bret and Steve followed Rita to the office and stood. Samantha then walked over to her desk and took a seat. Rita left and went into the copy-and-print room. Samantha then gazed at them, saying, "So, I heard Monica and you two have to go to court?" Bret and Steve nodded in agreement with the comment. Bret replied, "Boss, I don't know what else to tell you. We can't really talk about it." Samantha then raised her hand, stopping Bret, saying, "All right, all right. It's none of my business, but how is Monica involved is my question? That's the part that worries me. When is the court date?" Steve answered, "The hearing is Monday. Boss? …. You're not worried about us?" Samantha, then rolling her eyes at the remark, said, "Back to work, you two !"

Bret and Steve then came out of her office real quick. Steve sarcastically said, "Are we late? I don't know boss. One of these days, I'll give it back to her !" Bret laughed at the remark, not knowing Samantha heard what was said. She then got up from the seat and quickly yelled, "STEVE !" They both turned around and saw Samantha come out of the office, staring at the two of them. Samantha, putting both hands on her hips, responded, "Two things, LaBranche! One, I am still your boss and two, I will be accepting interns soon! ….If I were you, I'd be careful, just saying." They then watched her slowly go back into the office. They then walked to the breakroom. Bret saw no one else in the breakroom. He ignored what was said and replied, "She's the boss. It's Samantha's late, I mean way. Right?" They both were laughing around a table and took a seat for a break. Samantha hearing this said, "I heard that, Bret! ….Rita! …. Rita! Where are you?" Rita then ran out of the copy-and-print room, holding a folder under her arm, answering, "Coming !" Samantha then met with Rita in the hallway, giving her car keys saying, "I left my purse in the car. Can you get my purse for me? I have a million things to do." Rita then walked away, answering, "Ok, I'll be back".

Meanwhile, thirty minutes later at the De Nino residence, they were all still eating breakfast and talking. Sylvester stared at Monica, glad nothing had happened to her. He then glanced at Renee's hand over Feng's. Mario stood at the door, about to leave. He then looked back at everyone and asked, "How was breakfast?" They all answered, "Very good !" Renee watched Mario open and close the door, taking a sip of apple juice and saying, "I see why you have him come twice a week, Pop." They all laughed at the remark, then Feng said, "So, the next time you stop by, is he coming too?" They all laughed again, then Sylvester looked back at Monica and said, "You know I gotta thank your co-workers for saving my oldest."

Monica said, "Aaawww, Pop ! You're gonna make me cry." Renee had their godfather Bird in mind and asked, "Pop, should we tell Bird or …? Bird would want to be there for Chi Chi at the court trial." Sylvester answered, "I understand why your mother and I made him godfather for you both, but. …. I think you should pass on this one." Sylvester then glanced at Feng, getting up from the table and saying, "Feng, did you know these two girls can dance? We all used to dance a lot when they were younger." Sylvester, getting ironic, went on to say, "Like before Renee had dyed her hair blonde !" They all laugh at what was said but Renee; she then rolled her eyes at the comment made. Sylvester then looked at the girls and said, "Listen, the reason I spoke about dancing was to celebrate and get your mind off last night."

Monica took a sip of water from her cup, then got up and walked to the living room. She reached for the remote at the table and turned the TV on for music. Monica then found a music channel and looked back at her father, saying, "Pop, let's get down !" Sylvester then got up and joined Monica dancing together, having fun. She grabbed his hand dancing goofy all around him, smiling. Monica then glanced at Renee with Feng and replied, "Come on, you two. Grab the little mic, Renee ! It's on the couch." Renee then held Feng's hand and went into the living room. She then grabbed the mic from the couch and lip sang while dancing. Feng laughed at Renee being funny replied, "You come here a lot !" They all laughed together at the comment dancing to the music.

Carmen, early that afternoon, sat alone in a jail cell, resting his eyes. He reflected on his mother and himself very young visiting the church again. The cell door then opened and there stood a detective named Mike with a cop. Carmen then woke up and gazed at them. Mike, watching him, asked, "Mr. Lagaipa, can I talk to you?" Carmen then got up and walked out of the cell. The cop then checked him out and walked behind them. Carmen, with sarcasm, looked back at the cop asked, "Am I going home?" The detective laughed at Carmen and said, "Let's see what kind of deal we can make, right?" Carmen then went into a room with Mike. There sat another detective named Boddy, ready to talk with the previous photo at the table. Bobby then watched the cop open and close the door. He then stared at Carmen seated and said, "So, we have people testifying against you. Not one person, but people." Carmen then looked away, avoiding gossip. Mike, standing, waved at him and yelled, "HEY BUBBY, WE'RE OVER HERE !"

Bobby then continued on and reached for the photo, saying, "You tried to kidnap this beautiful, young lady. Not only her but her sister, if given the opportunity . .... Mike, am I wrong?" Mike shook his head no and asked a question, "Why?" Carmen proudly looked up at them and answered, "The kidnapping never happened; these are just lies." Mike glanced at Bobby and said, "Lies? ... Lies like putting a gun to a man's head, you're not gonna get away with this." Bobby then looked at the photo and said, "Speaking of a gun, there were guns with no license. I'm talking about you and your so-called friends." Mike waited for Carmen to answer but he didn't. Mike then asked, "So, if you weren't trying to kidnap, then why did you put a gun to this man's head?" Carmen, being aggravated, then shouting, "I WANT MY LAWYER ! GIVE ME MY LAWYER !" Bobby and Mike immediately walked out of the room, then stood and gossip in the hallway about the fate of Carmen.

Later that day, Sylvester drove his car and Feng followed him to the building parked next to each other. Monica, with her purse, Renee, and Feng got out of the SUV and couldn't get over the size of the building. Sylvester then got out of the car with the key, smiled, and asked, "You like what you see? A lot of space we have. This building is 4, 700 square feet and has two offices, plenty of parking space as you can see." Sylvester then walked over to the door and unlocked it. They all went inside and walked around the place. Monica, looking up at the white walls and black marble floor, asked, "Pop, where will your office be?" Sylvester replied, "In the back." Renee, holding Feng's hand, went left of the building, amazed of the space. Sylvester watched them and says, "What a nice office building, right? …. Imagine if we had a second floor."

Monica then walked up to her father said, "The wait is over, right?" Sylvester then gazed at Monica, still looking around the building. Sylvester then asked, "Is there any way I could get you girls to move in with me?" Monica glanced at her father, knowing he still wasn't over what could have happened to her. Monica smiled and answered, "We are fine, Pop. Plus, Grandpa gave Renee and I the house." Sylvester looked down, respecting Monica's answer and then back at her, saying, "All right. This is a new Chapter in our lives. I am looking to hire a lot of people by the way." Sylvester had her full attention, then went on to say, "Beautiful place, don't you think? Your mother's last painting will be here also." Monica got excited about the remark says, "Ma would had love this. … This place is beautiful ! I gotta tell Renee about Mom's last painting coming here !" Renee then glanced at her sister and father shouting, "COME CHECK THE SPACE OVER ON THIS SIDE, YOU GUYS !"

Monica, with Sylvester, came and focused on the space, wondering what to do with it. Feng then asked, "When are you looking to open the art gallery?" Sylvester stood and watched them walk around and answered, "Real soon. I have to hire and such." Sylvester then looked at his daughters with an idea asked, "Monica, would you and your sister mind decorating this place?" Renee began rolling her eyes at the remark replied, "Don't ask Monica to do the decorating because she will have this place looking very Italian and less universal." Sylvester thought about her comment and said, "Good point. Renee, you do the decorating. Monica, you'll be a manager." Renee then watched Monica feel joyful and speechless, saying, "Congrats, Chi Chi ! I don't want that headache." Feng, Renee, and Monica hugged in celebration of everything. The thought then hit Monica that she had to leave Samantha's Way. Sylvester then gazed at Feng, saying, "Feng, there is room for you here if you'd like." Feng smiled at the comment and replied, "I'm going to college so I can't." Sylvester then nodded, looking at Renee and saying, "Renee, you got yourself a smart man I see."

Renee got over excited thinking on how to decorate the place and asked, "When can I start, Pop?" Sylvester, glad to see Renee excited, replied, "I have the key to the building, so it all falls on you. The budget is twenty thousand dollars before you ask me. I will write the check out. You just let me know what you have in mind regarding the decoration. Ok?" Renee, ready to start, said, "I gotta look around. We might need a little more than twenty thousand, Pop !" Monica with Sylvester watched them leave with a mind to decorate. Sylvester then yelled, "TWENTY THOUSAND, RENEE! …. ALSO, I WILL NEED YOUR HELP ON HIRING THE RIGHT AMOUNT OF FLAVOR !" Monica looked at her father, chuckling at the comment says, "The right amount of flavor? … Let me guess, Mario. Right?" Sylvester then laughed at Monica while looking around.

Feng with Renee drove to a party store for the art gallery. Renee then opened the glove compartment, reaching for her shades, putting them on, saying, "I can't wait; I can't wait to start, love. You should have taken the job, working for my father. It's guaranteed, you know." Feng then stopped at a stop light on red and glanced at Renee closing the glove compartment. Feng said, "I'm good. When I go to college and come back, you and I … you know." Renee, not understanding, replying, "No. I don't know; what are you saying?" Feng looked away and said, "Renee, I don't need your father's help. I can provide for us by going to college." Renee then reached for his hand, and they both connect and kissed. Renee understood then and asked, "So, when do you want me to see your folks again?" The light then turned green and Feng answered, "Soon I guess; they like you. And thanks for looking out for me." Renee smiled and realized they were getting closer to the party store. Feng made a left turn, driving into the plaza.

After parking, they came inside and saw it was busy. They then went straight to the nearest register and stood next to a lady being served. The customer reached and placed her bags into the cart and gazed at them. Renee, with a purse, removed her shades and made eye contact, getting rude, said, "Sometime today, lady !" The lady then paid the cashier and frowned at the remark. She watched Renee roll her eyes while leaving. Renee then looked at the cashier and said, "Listen, I need you or someone else to help us out, pronto. ... I have a lot to do !"

The cashier said, "I will send a co-worker to help you out. What aisle by the way?" Feng then glanced up at the aisle chart and saw decoration was in aisle five. Feng replied, "Aisle five." They then walked into aisle five, looking around. Feng gazed at Renee weird because of the disrespect she gave. Feng said, "Renee, you could lighten up. You were rude to a lady, now a cashier? We can do our own shopping." Renee heard him out, then replied, "I know; it's just I want to do this right." Feng answered, "Your father won't let you fail, you know this." Renee then rested her head on his shoulder, knowing he was right. She then saw the cashier. They spoke with point in their direction, sending three workers. One of the employees quickly came over to them, asking, "How can I help you both?" It then hit Renee that they left Monica. Renee then stood straight and quickly reached into the purse for her phone. Renee immediately called Monica, looking to the right at glittery hearts in different colors. Renee then handed Feng her shades and reached for the middle shelf holding a glittery blue heart.

Monica answered, "Renee?" Renee looked away from the help, saying, "Sorry, we left you, Chi Chi ; clearly I wasn't thinking ! We are headed back to get you." Feng gazed at Renee with the three employees waiting on them.

Monica, at the time, stood near the entry door asked, "Where are you?" Feng then raised his index finger as a signal to the workers to wait on them. Renee then put back the heart replied, "We're at a party store on Lake Avenue." Sylvester then came from the back into the main room and saw Monica on the phone. He heard their conversation walking over. Monica had zoned out, not hearing her father walk from behind, and went on to say, "Since you're there on Lake Avenue, can you get me a banana-and-strawberry shake?" Renee chuckled and answered, "That's not a problem. Question, are we going back for you because Pop is there?" Monica finally turned around and saw her father standing close from behind, so she asked, "Pop, you mind giving me a ride home? I was supposed to go with them, but I'd much rather go back home." Sylvester replied, "Of course I will, are you ready?" Monica said, "You must had been in your office because I didn't see you five minutes ago." Renee, waiting on an answer, said, "Hello?"

Monica answered, "Yeah, Pop is giving me a ride back home so forget the shake." Renee then hung up, walking with Feng and the three workers looking for a style that suited the building. Sylvester then locked up with Monica, leaving the building. They then got inside his car and drove away. Monica then reached into the purse to finds her shades. She then put them on, watching the cars go by. After driving for ten minutes, they reached the house only to pass it. Monica glanced at her father and said, "Pop, you miss the house. ….Where are we going?" Sylvester smiled at the remark and answered, "How about that banana strawberry shake you love?" Monica got excited and sarcastically said, "You care about me; you really care about me !" They laughed as he made a right turn into the plaza where the milk shake store was.

Later that day, Renee with Feng came out of the store with three shopping carts' worth of supplies. The three workers help load the SUV up with Feng; Renee sat in the passenger seat checking her phone. Renee said, "There is another store I want to check, love !" After they finished, they each received a ten-dollar tip from Feng. The workers were grateful and thanked Feng for the tip, walking way. Feng then opened the door and got inside, ready to take off. Feng glanced at Renee, knowing she wanted to go to another store. Feng held the keys asking, "Why do you want to go to another store? … Renee, you already spent fifteen hundred at this place. You can't be serious?" Renee annoyedly answered, "Feng ! This is gonna be my career. Can you be more supportive? You know, like supportive ! ….Seriously, you can start the truck up." Feng inhaled, then exhaled and started up the SUV, saying, "All right, all right you win. Give the recipe to your father in regards to the budget." Renee smiled, ready to shop for the entire evening.

Two days later, on a Monday at 10 am, was the hearing in the courtroom. The De Ninos with Feng were there. The plaintiff and defendant were ready; Monica's lawyer Casey and Carmen's lawyer named Ricky. Carmen's mother Stephanie was there, seated close and watching. Casey finally meeting Monica, Bret, and Steve, greeting them with a handshake. Casey then sat down and went over a few things. When Judge Michael Hammond came out and was announced, everyone was told to stand by the court orderly. The hearing began. Within a half hour, the judge then was provided enough evidence from Casey. Casey spoke on attempted murder, their old photo provided by an officer for identifying the girls, and a possible kidnapping plot to move forward in the case. Ricky's last comments were, "If the kidnapping was true, why did Monica agree to date Carmen then? Why didn't Carmen kidnap her when they recently saw each other?" The judge then called for a trial date on July 16. The judge then got up, and the court orderly saw and told all to rise as the judge left. Everyone stood and watched the judge leave, then was dismissed. Monica then looked at her father, grateful the evil plots didn't happen. Casey saw and said, "Monica, you and the fellas have nothing to worry about. At the trial, you will be asked to testify. Enjoy the rest of your day." Monica nodded, watching Casey meet and speak with Sylvester.

Chapter 8

The Giant Step Forward !

The next day later, on a windy afternoon, Monica was home alone sitting on the couch in the living room watching TV. Monica then held the remote up, turning the channel to a drama with a woman going on her lunch break, catching her boyfriend kissing another woman in a hallway at their job. Monica watched the girlfriend standing outside an office, surprised, then ran over to beat him up with her purse. The boyfriend apologized, then fell backwards, blocking the purse. Monica laughed, saying, "Get him, girl ! Wait? Where is the girl he kissed?" Monica then saw the girlfriend run after the lady. She continued to laugh at the situation. Monica then glanced at the living room table and saw her phone and no mail, then she put down the remote. Monica then got up from the couch and went outside to the mailbox. She checked and saw two catalogs for Renee and a letter in regards to the court date. Monica opened the letter and read it, wanting to get it over with. Shre had brought the mail inside, not in the mood for court at all. She then placed the mail down at the living room table. The moment she sat down at the couch, her phone began to ring. She then reached for the phone from the table and saw it was Laura, her co-worker.

Monica answered and said, "Laura, what's doing? Are you working right now?" Laura replied, "No, I'm home in the kitchen right now. Are you busy?" Monica got curious and reached for the remote, turning the volume down, then put the remote back and answered, "No. Samantha told me to come in tomorrow by a text message. So, I haven't been back to work yet. What's up?" Laura said, "Monica, I don't know how else to say this, but. ….I am nervous. I am really nervous, I gotta tell ya. You're a good friend and give good advice. I mean we all get nervous sometimes. Right?" Monica, not understanding, immediately replied, "Laura, you wanna tell me what you're nervous about?"

Laura then took a breather and answered, "I'm a comedian. Today is my first time on stage and I am really nervous, Monica. Monica?" The comment took Monica by surprise. Monica then answered, "I heard ya. Who'd thought a quiet secretary would be a comedian. Right?" Laura laughed at the remark and said, "I believe I can be funny, Monica, but I never told jokes in front of a live audience before, not even my family." Monica asked, "Could you tell me a joke right now?" Laura, with joy in her voice, replied, "You know what; I can with you. I feel comfortable joking with you for some reason." Monica said, "So, tell me a joke then." Laura took another breather and said, "So, I can't find love. Right? I been single for a good seven years. I know I am a big girl, but I need love too. I need to start a website and show these men who's boss; nothing dirty though. I'm talking a website that would make the skinniest girl want to be me and their men downloading my app."

Monica laughed at the comment and said, "Laura, I think you can do better. It was funny but really seven years?.. What would your app be named?" Laura answered, "Yeah, seven long years and counting. Lopiano Tano would be my app !" Monica laughed and said, "That was funny ! Did you just make that up?" Laura replied, "I did indeed. What would your app be called, Monica?" Monica thought about it and answered, "Probably … Chi Chi Nino !" They both started laughing at the names they came up with. Monica said, "I guess I have to loosen you up first, right? You're performing tonight?" Laura quickly answered, "Yes, I am. I was already informed what I can and can't say on stage; nothing racist or really inappropriate. You know racism is like quicksand; it keeps ya stuck. So, anyways will you be there?" Monica then got up from the couch and said, "Yeah, I will come out to see your first act. When and where?" Laura answered, "Seven o'clock at that comedy club on 101 Cathy Street in downtown New Haven. I'm the opening act." Monica then said, "Alright, now let's go over the rest of your jokes right now. After we finish your jokes, you should have everyone laughing and wanting to come see you again." Laura, with much excitement, replied, "Let's get started !"

Monica suddenly heard a vehicle pull up behind her car. She then went over to the blinds and saw it Feng with Renee. Feng turned the engine off, then opened the door talking to Renee. Renee got out of the SUV with her purse, and slammed the door, walking away anger. Feng, not liking her giving any answer, said, "So, you're not gonna talk to me? Renee?" Feng watched her go straight to the door ignoring him. Feng locked the SUV, then walked behind her frustrated. Monica then opened the door and glanced at her sister coming inside, asking, "Renee, you ok?" Renee gave no answer, facing the door. She then threw her purse on the couch, waiting for Feng to come inside.

The moment Feng came inside and closed the door back, Renee then got in his face, asking, "Who was she? Don't you lie to me, Feng !" Feng answered, "I don't know that lady; you and I were together the whole day. You don't trust me?" Renee quickly responded, "Trust you? I do trust you, Feng; it's just why? Why would some random girl walk up to you, giving her number right in front of me? Why?" Feng then glanced at Monica, crossing her arms with the phone, disappointed in the situation. Laura, still on the phone, said, "Monica ! ... Hello?" Monica heard her and replied, "Laura, I will call you right back. Ok?" Monica then hung up and, with a serious look, asked, "Are you cheating on my sister?" Feng frowned at the remark and answered, "No, Monica. Some lady today lusted after me at this decoration store was all. Renee was right there with me and … And." Monica yelled," AND WHAT?" Renee then answers, "We're not allowed back in that store, Monica. The lady and I got into a fight." Monica got surprised and asked, "And what did Feng do?" Feng answered, "I got into it with the store manager on the situation. I crumbed and threw away her number on paper." Monica then glanced at her sister, saying, "Well, he didn't cheat on you. You ok?" Renee began to cross her arms, looking away and, in a soft voice, replied, "I didn't like it. "

Feng then walked up to Renee, saying, "That girl was making trouble, you know this." Renee answers, "Yeah, yeah I guess. I just didn't like it." Feng said, "After you too then fought, I don't think she likes you either." Renee laughed at the remark, then hugged him and replied, "Forget about her; I apologize for putting you through this." Feng then asked, "So, where did you learn how to fight like that?" Renee smiled and said, "Kung fu movies." Monica watched them get along, then headed to her room to call Laura back.

Later that evening at 6:45 pm, Monica had arrived and parked across the street from the comedy club. Monica locked the car doors, dressed casually with her purse and wearing dark shades. Monica looked at the people waiting in a long line with the thought being, *I should had left earlier.* Monica then walked, looking both ways, and crossed the street, joining the line and stood last. Monica then went through her purse for her phone, then immediately the head of security came out yelling, "IS THERE A MONICA, LAST NAME DE NINO, HERE?" Monica, excited, raised her arm high, waving at him. He saw, then pointed at her standing away from the line and said, "You, come inside." Monica then cut the line and met with the man while the people began to gossip about her.

The head of security then asked for Monica's ID. She then reached into her purse and handed it to him. He then looked at the ID and handed it back, saying, "Follow me; Laura wants you." Monica then followed him inside among the crowd, passing the bar and headed to an opened door next to the stage to a hallway. They then showed up at Laura's door. He knocked and said, "Laura, your friend Monica is here." Laura yelled, "COME INSIDE !" He then opened and closed the door for Monica. She saw Laura sitting around the mirror nervous. Laura then got up from the chair and they hugged. Monica watched her take a breather. Monica asked, "Still nervous?" Laura answered, "I am, I don't know. I do know I don't have that much time. You look good, Monica." Monica then removed her shades and smiled at the remark, saying, "And you, yourself. Once you get out there, you'll be fine. Who's the closing act and how long are you gonna be on stage?" Laura, watching Monica put the shades in her purse, replied, "I got five minutes on stage. The guy that's closing name is Larry Cole, some comedian from New Jersey." They then heard a knock at the door, hearing a man's voice say, "Laura, it's time !" Laura glanced at the door and said, "Here goes nothing. Right? I told them to save you a seat up front." Monica, surprised, answered, "You didn't have to do that, seriously. Well, let me let you go. Say a prayer before you go on stage. Ok?" They both hugged again, then Monica walked out of the room, closing the door. Monica then walked the hallway where a security guard stood and held the door to the main room opened for her.

Laura then heard another knock at the door. She wondered who it was this time, so she asked, "Who it is?" She heard another man's voice say, "Laura, It's Larry Cole. Listen, I hope you do well tonight." Laura then opened the door only to see Larry standing with two shot glasses filled with alcohol. Laura then questioned him, asking, "You're drinking before your act?" Larry stood by the door, laughing at the comment, and answered, "I do; it helps me out on stage. These shots are for my wife and I. You look nervous, Laura; take a shot." Larry then handed her a glass, saying, "Take it to calm ya down." Laura then took the shot, swallowing it down and then handing him back the glass. Laura then made a sour face due to the alcohol being strong. She then glanced at him, asking, "What was in that shot?" Larry laughed again, replying, "Before I go on stage, I normally ask the bartender for something strong, so I don't know. I wish you the best out there." Laura then watched Larry walk to his room down the hall. She then stood and waited for the host to call her up. Monica, at the time, sat in the front row to the left, looking around. She then saw Rita about to take a seat two rows behind among the crowd. Rita then held her phone up, recording like the audience did. She got excited, now seeing Monica. The host named Luke then came out from the back to the stage to start the show.

Luke took the microphone from the stand, then glanced around and said, "Are you all ready to get this show started?" The audience all shouted, "YEAH !" Luke said, "That's what I want to hear. All right, first up is a comedian who I think is funny. This is her first time here on stage. Everyone, give a round of applause for the one and only, Laura Lopiano !" Luke then put back the microphone on the stand and walked, passing Laura coming out. Laura then removed the microphone from the stand, making eye contact with Monica recording her by phone and smiling. Laura asked, "How is everybody doing tonight?" The audience got excited and cheered her on. Laura then walked to the left and saw a happy couple in front. She then made eye contact with them, asking, "Are you both happy?" The couple nodded and answered yes. The lady laughed at Laura. Laura then said, "Wait, I haven't started with a joke yet !" The audience had begun to laugh at the comment. Laura asked, "How many years have you two been together?" The guy answers,

"Two years !" Laura said, "Glad you both are happy, honestly. Wish I could say the same thing, yeah. I though my ex was it for me. Of course, we lived together. He was unemployed he would eat all my food and gave me an attitude like I deserved it." The audience began to laugh at the comment and Laura said, "Like my birthday, he's asking me what kind of cake I'm buying? I'm like seriously, I got to buy my own cake on my birthday ! So, asking for candles would be too much to ask. Right?"

The audience laughed, watching her walk to the right. She then shrugged her shoulder and said, "And everything's a question with this guy. I can't take him nowhere. Some random guy came up to us outside a store one day, asking for directions. My ex says, 'What am I, a tourist guide' and curses the man out ! ... They told me to keep it clean on stage, folks!" The audience laughed watching her move around. Laura then laughed and said, "I can go on and on about my ex but …. I want to talk about treating people right for a second." The audience then applauded for a minute on the statement, then she said, "Treat people right. I so happened to work under the leadership of a bimbo that thinks otherwise. Right? Who runs a business where the co-workers won't come to work because of the boss? ….Yeah, we're always hiring." The audience laughed, watching her stand tall and say, "If I ran that company, it would rock. I don't know how but it would. Treat people right, right? Hopefully I can do this for a living before my job sinks and everything in it. I am Laura Lopiano and you all have been great, thank you !" The audience applauded, watching her put back the microphone on the stand, leaving the stage. Luke then came out again ready to introduce another comedian.

Monica then stopped recording the performance and received a text message from Laura, saying, "Come to the back." Monica then saw a different security guard wave at her from the right side, pointing at the door she came from. Monica, watching Luke leave the stage, then grabbed her purse and headed to the door, being escorted by the security guard. A comedian named, Russell then came to the stage, looking at the audience, then Monica. Russell, lusting after her, said, "What a beautiful, young lady. I see you're going to the back, miss !" Monica then looked up at the comedian and stopped. The guard told her to follow him. Russell chuckled and said, "I can see why you have a free pass to the back, sweetie. I'll be done in a minute !" Monica then stopped again and heard the crowd laugh at her. She frowned at Russell, asking," What's your deal?" The security guard calmly guided her to the door, saying, "Ignore him and follow me." Monica then followed the security guard, now hearing the audience laugh at a joke said about a couple in the front row.

Laura was in her room, taking another shot with Larry, laughing at a joke said at that time. Larry's wife named Katie was looking for him, passing the hallway. Katie then saw the door open and spotted her husband drinking. She then went into the room, saying, 'Hun, for the past five minutes I was looking for you." Larry then apologized to his wife and introduce Laura to her. His wife then glanced at the shot glass he held. Katie began to worry and said, "Larry, that's enough. You're closing, remember?" Larry nodded his head in agreement and said, 'Alright Laura, I gotta get ready. You did good out there." Laura smiled and said, "Thank you." Laura then watched them leave the room. She then took a seat, looking into the mirror.

Monica then showed up at her room, walking over and saying," Wow, Laura you were something else out there." Laura then got up from her seat and answered, "Thanks to you, girl. I guess we will see what happens on them inviting me back, right?" Monica immediately smelled the alcohol through her breath and nodded at the comment, saying, "I am sure they will invite you back. Rita was out there; did you see her?" Laura, caught by surprised, answered, "You saw Rita? Really? No, I didn't see her. What do you think?" Monica began to cross her arms, saying, "I don't know yet. I had recorded you though. I have your first performance on stage. You were very confident out there … as if you've done this before." When Laura heard those words, she felt extremely confident in her craft, saying, 'Thank you for being there for me." They then hugged out of excitement. Monica then asked, "Could ya do me a small favor?"

Laura, amazed, said, "What's up?" Monica then replied, "The comedian after you, if you could roast him for me?" Laura laughed at the remark and agreed to roast Russell. Monica and Laura stayed at the club for the entire evening for Larry's performance. When Larry came to the stage, he gave lots of laughter and made everyone's evening.

Monica was called in early for work the next morning. She arrived ready and on time. Monica got out of the car, wearing makeup, with dark shades, in a blue designer dress with her purse. Monica then locked her car and gazed at the building, with the thought of Why do I put up with this place. When Monica came inside, Rita said, "Welcome back, Monica, come." Rita at the time was in conversation with Samantha, standing outside the office. Monica then walked over and glanced at the secretary desk, seeing no one there. Monica then asked, "Where is Laura?" Samantha, seated in the office, heard her voice and asked, "Rita, is that Monica? "Rita replied, "Yes." Monica then went into Samantha's office, looking around smelling peach from a spray can on the desk. Monica then watched Samantha signal Rita to close the door. Samantha, smiling at Monica, said, "I thank you for coming in earlier. How was your vacation? "Monica answered, "It was ok; nothing crazy though. Is Laura here today?" Samantha began folding her hands together and made eye contact with Rita. Samantha then glanced back at Monica and replied, "I called you in early because I need your help. You will be doing the secretary work until I hire someone. I fired Laura over the phone this morning. You wanna know why, right?" Monica asked, "Are Bret and Steve still working here or?" Samantha chuckled at the comment, saying, "That's not what I asked you !" Rita looked away out of shame and focused on the door. Monica then glanced at Rita and understood by her mood. Monica began to laugh at Samantha and answered, "You couldn't take a joke, could you/ So, you just fired her like that without a warning?"

Samantha then got up and stood over her desk, saying, "What Laura did was bad for my business; it's bad enough we're always hiring." Monica, disappointed in her decision, said, "She hasn't one time mentioned your name or your business. I have the video to prove it." Samantha then got anger with her, defending Laura, and yelled, "PEOPLE KNOW HER AND KNOW WHERE SHE WORKS AT, MONICA ! I AM PRETTY SURE WHAT SHE SAID IS ONLINE NOW ! …. AND I CAN'T TAKE ANY CHANCES AT ALL!" Samantha had calmed down and then, in a softer tone of voice, said," "Monica, don't quit on me; please don't. I need your help." Samantha then sat back down, watching Monica's reaction to the situation. She then looked at the applications on her desk, putting them in order. Monica, out of frustration, said, "I am here to help. I don't agree with you firing her. Write-ups are more understandable !" Samantha, with a serious look, yelled, "MONICA, SHE'S FIRED; IT'S OVER ! …. AND I DON'T WANNA ARGUE OR LOSE YOU OVER THIS! ….

THIS IS SAMANTHA'S WAY ! ... AND YOU NEED TO RESPECT MY RULES ! ... I AM DONE !" Samantha then gave a hand signal for Rita to open the door. Monica then removed and held her shades, glancing at the door. Samantha chuckled and said, "You look good, Monica. Thanks again for coming in today. Rita will show you what to do in regards to secretary work."

Monica left the office with Rita, still upset. They then walked over to the secretary desk and made eye contact. Monica then asked, "Rita, why did you go and tell Samantha? She didn't mention Samantha's name or job." Rita then took a breather and answered, "I felt it was the right thing to do. She made us look really bad on stage. Lopiano is a grown woman; she knew what she was doing." Monica, being sarcastic, said, "She fired Laura but kept Bret and Steve, right? Rita, that makes no sense at all !" Rita then warned Monica that Samantha's door was still opened and to calm down. Monica then shrugged her shoulders and replied, "Rita, I really don't care at this point !" Samantha indeed heard the statement and got up from her desk, frowning. Monica then turned around and saw Samantha with her arms crossed, looking back at her. Rita wondering what Monica was looking at, turned and saw Samantha upset. Samantha then said, "Monica, I am tired of you talking about this situation. I don't wanna hear it again ! ... Rita, tell Troy I want to see him now !" Rita went immediately on a search for Troy, walking the hallway. Monica began frowning at the comment and walked up to her, saying, "You're gonna do something?" Samantha quickly answered, "Of course I'm gonna do something. I am still your boss, Monica !" The coworkers heard and all came out into the hallway, watching. Samantha saw and continued on with Monica, saying, "Take the day off, Monica !" Monica then put her shades back on, leaving the office upset. Rita and Troy made their way through the co-workers and met with Samantha. Samantha watched Monica leave and yelled, "GET BACK TO WORK, EVERYONE ! … TROY, IN MY OFFICE !" Troy went in and waited inside the office while Samantha and Rita gossiped about Monica's actions.

Monica finally showed up home and parked, sitting in her car for a few minutes. She then made her mind up to quit the job. Monica then called and spoke with Laura over the phone. She wanted to hire her as an employee for the art gallery. Laura declines on the offer and wanted to pursue a career as a comedian. They both stayed in touch and remained good friends. After a few days of Monica not coming to work, Samantha understood, then terminated her job. Renee then began to put ads out online in regards to hiring artists, art agents, art consultants, art dealers, art valuers, art auctioneers, and a secretary for the art gallery. Renee also made time to decorate the art gallery, keeping things real simple. People immediately responded to the ad in and out of state. Monica received a lot of submissions and questions in regards to those careers. Sylvester then gave his daughters the date, location, and time to schedule the interviews immediately.

Monica with Renee interviewed all candidates on a Saturday, from 9 am to 7 pm, at the art gallery building a week before the court date. The job fair was incredibly crowded inside and out. Sylvester was there in his office reviewing applications. They're stood two armed security guards at the entry door inside. Sylvester, Monica, and Renee later made some hard decisions receiving 2, 998 applications that evening. Renee called and hired the chosen employees two days later. Sylvester, within days of the trial date, had the art gallery have a commercial with him talking for the exposure. The commercial caught the attention of many at that time in and out of state.

On the trial day at 10:00 am on a Monday morning, July 16, 2018, in the courtroom, the De Ninos with Feng sat down together in the uncrowded public seating area. Behind them sat the officers that made the arrest. Monica, Bret, Steve, and Casey, her lawyer, sat at the plaintiff's table. Casey went over a few things in regards to letting him lead. Ben, Victor, Carmen, and his lawyer, Ricky, sat to the right. Carmen's mother, with her fiancée named Vin sat behind Carmen. They were hoping things worked out in Carmen's favor, watching him turned around and smile at them. Ben glanced at the jury, then Victor in disgust, asking, "Why?" Victor ignored Ben, waiting for the judge to come out. The judge then came into the room and the court orderly said, "All rise in honor for Judge Michael Hammond. This court is now in session !" Everyone in the courtroom stood for the judge. The judge gazed around, then sat down. The court orderly then said, "You may be seated. The people of the state of Connecticut verses Mr. Carmen Lagaipa, Mr. Ben Ricci, and Mr. Victor Roman." The judge watch everyone sit, then received a folder from the court orderly. He opened and reviewed it for a few minutes, then said, "I have a case with the defendants, Mr. Carmen Lagaipa, Mr. Ben Ricci …. Mr. Victor Roman, I see you are testifying against Mr. Lagaipa in the involvement of attempt to kidnap, attempted murder, assault and battery, stalking and illegal fire arms." Victor stood up and answered, "Yes, your honor." The judge looked at Victor and said, "You may be seated." Carmen avoided eye contact with the judge. Ricky took notice and frowned, then softly said, "Carmen, it looks bad when you don't give the judge your full attention." Carmen glanced at Ricky, then under his breath said, "Get me outta here." The judge continued on and said, "Ok, so there are four that are testifying against you Mr. Lagaipa." Ricky, being ready, got up and asked, "Your honor, can I go first?" The judge, with a serious look, shook his head no and said, "I'd like to hear from the first witness. Mr. Bevans, would you come to the witness stand? Is Monica here?" The court orderly pointed to the left at the end, watching her stand up. The judge then stared at her for a moment and said, "You may be seated." Monica then sat down and looked at her father, confused, then under her voice mumbled, "Carmen and his lawyer is a joke. How can he save him? Bunch of canaries, they are !"

Bret then came to the witness stand and took a seat. After being given the oath, he was asked questions from Ricky in regard to what had happened. Ricky walked and stood near Bret, asking," Mr. Bevans, was Mr. Lagiapa defending himself from an attack?" Bret answered, "No. Steve and I were attacked after not agreeing with him in regards to the kidnapping. Had it not been for the cops, I would have been dead." Ricky then asked," Why did Mr. Lagaipa invite you to his office?" Bret then glanced at Carmen smirking at him replied, "He mentioned about a party and an open position at his job; nothing to do with a kidnapping." Ricky asked, 'Do you know Mr. Lagaipa? Bret answered, "Yes. We went to the same high school together: him, Steve, and I." Ricky then asked, "The gun fired. Was that you involved in wanting to shoot Mr. Laigaipa? …. Explaining why Mr. Laigaipa stood over you . …. This is what the cops witnessed, am I right?" Bret shook his head no and answered, "Yes, the cops witnessed him standing over me. I never touched a gun; my fingerprints weren't even on the gun !" After hearing from Bret, the judge had told him to go back to his seat. The judge then began to ask Ricky a question about Carmen's behavior. Ricky answered standing before the judge and told him that Carmen had mental issues due to the abuse of his father and not letting go of a promise about a better life. Ricky then replied,"All he needed was help to solve these issues." Ricky then glanced at Ben, thinking on a way to save him. Ben kept his head down the entire time. The judge then looked down at a few documents and asked, "Did the defendants know anything about a will?" Ricky answered, "Yes, your honor." The judge then said, "You may be seated." The judge then wanted to hear from Casey. Casey then stood and spoke up for his team, providing the document of Dean's will he replied, "I now have this document. I've no need to question Carmen or Ben, your honor. Carmen was after their money by any means necessary. Him knowing the family made Miss. De Nino feel strangely comfortable; maybe because he is handsome. I don't know, Your Honor. Mr. LaBranche's life was in danger as well. Ben and Victor attacking him almost witnessing a murder, Your Honor." The judge then glanced at the document given to him from the court orderly by Casey, saying, "You may be seated." Victor was called next to the witness stand and had testified against Carmen being questioned by Casey. Victor told the found address and plot, saying Carmen was the mastermind. Casey had no other questions and the judge told Victor he may be seated. Monica was asked very little from Casey as he sat down in regards to the date.

The judge then asked Casey, "Counsellor, did Miss. De Nino find it kind of odd Mr. Lagaipa wanting to date her immediately?" Casey stood up and answered, "No, Your Honor." The judge then glanced at Monica and Casey, saying," You may be seated." Monica was called next to the witness stand and was asked few questions from Ricky. Monica answered how they met years before. She agreed to go on a date and that Carmen never came off strange toward her. Ricky gazed at the judge and said, "I have no further question for her, Your Honor." The judge then gazed at Monica and said, "You may be seated." Steve was called last and had come to the witness stand and was asked very few questions by Ricky. Steve answered, "Yes, we were held at gunpoint by Ben against our will. Yes, I was held down by Victor and Ben." When Steve was asked about the two men by Ricky, he pointed at Victor and Ben. Ricky lastly asked, "The photo shown to you by Carmen. Were you sure it was Monica and her family, including Paul?" Steve answered, "Yes, I knew it was Monica based on the photo. Monica is who I know; nobody else in the photo." Ricky then looked at the judge and said, "I have no questions, Your Honor." The judge then looked at Steve and said, "You may be seated." The judge glanced at Casey, asking, "Mr. Logan, you have any other witnesses?" Casey stood up, looking back at the two officer that made the arrest. Casey felt no need to call them and replied, "No, Your Honor." The judge then said, "You may be seated."

The judge then read the will document for the De Nino family, saying,"Monica and Renee were given $2.5 million dollars each. The rest of the money went to Sylvester, Marie, and their son, leaving them $5 million dollars. Dean's home was left for his grandchildren." The judge then made his decision in regards to the case. The judge understood and saw that Bret, Steve, and Monica's lives were in danger. Victor was given six years with a bail of $65, 000 dollars for testifying. Ben had received eight years with a bail of $80, 000 dollars based on his involvement. Carmen was found guilty and had received twenty years facing all the charges without bail. Ricky couldn't get the judge to lessen the sentence, watching the jury agree. Carmen then heard his mother sadly yell out loud, "NO ! MY BABY; THEY CAN'T TAKE MY ONLY SON FROM ME !" Vin tried to keep her calm by hugging her and yelled, YOUR HONOR, TWENTY YEARS WITHOUT BAIL? THAT AIN'T FAIR, YOUR HONOR !" The judge then hit the gavel and yelled, "ORDER IN THE COURT, I SAID ORDER IN THE COURT !" The judge then gazed at Carmen and asked, "Any last words before I have you taken away, sir?" Carmen glances at Monica and said, "I did not intended to harm you or your family ….sorry." Ricky gazed at Carmen and Ben, saying, "I tried." The court orderly saw the judge rise and said, "All rise in honor as Judge Michael Hammond leaves !" Everyone stood up and watched this tall, grey-haired judge leave. Stephanie, crying, watched her son, Victor, and Ben being escorted by three officers. Stephanie then watched Casey hug Monica and got anger and left with Vin. Feng, with the De Ninos, met with Monica, Bret, and Steve. Bret and Steve surprised, had recognized Feng from the gas station and greeted him. Steve pointed at Feng, saying, "Gas station, the fight? …. You know the De Ninos?" Feng laughed at the comment and replied, "I was here at the hearing as well. I'm with Monica's sister; it's a small world, Right?" They all laughed at the remark. Casey then gazed at Sylvester and Monica hugging, saying, "Everything worked out fine like I told you." Sylvester replied, "Indeed. Thanks Logan." Sylvester then gazed at Bret and Steve, saying, "You two come with us and celebrate. I can't thank you guys enough for what you did." Bret and Steve were happy and agreed to come with the De Ninos to a restaurant to celebrate.

Two day later, in the evening time, at Vin and Stephanie's home in the suburbs of New Haven, Connecticut, Stephanie was still hurt about her son. She felt Carmen should have gotten a lesser sentence. She was in the kitchen washing dishes and heard Vin's footsteps. He then stood around the kitchen table, worried about her. Vin was a tall, shave-headed, and a caring guy. Vin said, "Listen, this is killing me. The past three years being together, we never not talked to one another ! You've been really quiet the past two days. You know I still love you, right?" Stephanie then stopped and turned the sink off. She turned and faced him, saying, "Yes, I know you do. I ... ." Vin, with a no-nonsense look, said, "I what?" Stephanie then began to shed tears. She went over and hugged him, saying, "I feel empty, like a part of me is leaving me ! Carmen is my only son, my only." Vin then reaches for some paper towels from the kitchen table. He ripped apart and handed it to her. After wiping her face, she said, "Sylvester is what caused this whole thing !"

Vin, not understanding, asked, "Who's Sylvester? Is he a friend of yours?" Stephanie shook her head no and replied, "No, no friend of mine. The young lady in court, her father's name is Sylvester. Paul, my ex-husband, and this guy would had been business partners years ago; both families know each other."

Vin knew where this was going. He took a breather and said, "I hear revenge when you talk. Let it go." When Stephanie heard the comment, she immediately walked away disappointed and yelled, "DON'T TALK TO ME OR TOUCH ME ! ... LET WHAT GO, TWENTY YEARS?" She then went into their bedroom and slammed the door closed. Vin then put both his hands on his hips, looking down in thought of what was said. Stephanie then made her mind up that by killing Sylvester, the De Nino family would feel her pain, even if it meant her life. Stephanie then came up with an idea to write a false letter out, admitting to have slept with Sylvester recently to create a feud. Stephanie thought to avoid sending a text message to delay things. Stephanie knew how much Vin loved her and would do anything for her. Stephanie then waited for the right day and time to leave the letter and get revenge.

August 14, 2018: Marie's Canaries had opened with eleven employees and a security guard in East Haven. The name Marie's Canaries was spelled big with a neon yellow glow. Sylvester was the gallery owner and Monica the sales manager. The three artists they hired, their work was very original and pleasing. Their names were Michael, Jerica, and Tristan. Marie's painting was the last one hung in a display case near the offices, showing two canary birds facing two different directions. Marie's Canaries provided two leather couches and 103 paintings for the people to view. The opening was crowded with two waiters around a long table, serving finger food and drinks in the middle near the entrance. Yellow canary balloons were all over in celebration.

Bret and Steve, at the time, continued working at Samantha's Way but were currently looking elsewhere for work until this day. Bird and Sylvester remained friends after a sit-down a day after the art gallery opened. They met at a restaurant in conversation, getting over the awkward feeling of them date the same woman; one being married to her and the other godfather to their children.

Chapter 9

When Revenge Visits !

ithin the opening week of Marie's Canaries on a Thursday afternoon, Stephanie, home alone, then decided to make her move that day, leaving the letter on their bed. Stephanie then opened and went into the closet, looking down and into a shoebox where her gun was and took it. Stephanie then closed the closet and put the gun inside her purse and left with the thought being, "May Father God forgive me." Shortly after, the De Ninos with Feng had left the house for lunch at a Italian restaurant in downtown New Haven. They were being followed by Stephanie. She remembered their address when Victor had testified in court. The De Ninos and Feng then arrived and were seated, dressed casually and having a good time talking about the future while eating breadsticks. Stephanie was in the parking lot inside her car, with the thought being, *You can do this, Steph* ! Stephanie then got out and locked the car, walking and opening her purse, crossing the street to the entrance.

Monica, at the time, was telling jokes. Everyone at the table was laughing at the jokes, waiting for their food. Monica said, "The judge says to Casey, did Miss. De Nino find it strange that Carmen wanted to date me immediately?" Monica, being sarcastic, continued on to say, "Your Honor, it's not every day that a pretty boy wants to kidnap me. I'm sorry, my money, right?" They all laughed at the table. Sylvester, after calming down from laughter, said, "I was worried about you, love."

Stephanie then came inside and saw it was crowded. She then went passed the waiters around the front desk. The waiters took notice and one followed her, asking, "Miss? Miss, can I help you?" Stephanie then saw the De Ninos and came closer to their table, passing the manager. Everyone stopped and watched her actions while being called miss a couple times. The De Ninos took notice as she stopped at their table, staring at Sylvester. Sylvester knew it was Stephanie. Sylvester replied, "Stephanie? It's been a minute since we've seen each other; what brings you here?" The manager then got in front of Stephanie and said, "Miss, please can I help you?" The manager then realized she was ignoring him, so, out of frustration, he pointed to the door and said, "Please leave, miss." Stephanie looked at the manager, then back at the De Ninos and out of anger yelled, "I

BET YOU ALL THINK SEEING MY SON GET SENTENCE TO TWENTY YEARS IS REAL FUNNY ! RIGHT?" The manager then shouted, "THAT'S IT ! I'M CALLING THE POLICE !" The manager then rushed to his office with the waiter and called 911.

Monica, feeling worried, then looked at her father and asked, "Is this Carmen's mom?" Stephanie then reached into her purse and pulled a gun out, pointing at Sylvester. The customers were stunned and speechless, watching the purse drop. Stephanie shouted, "HE CAN'T DO TWENTY YEARS; HE IS ALL I GOT AND YOU KNOW THIS ! …. I LOST MY HUSBAND AND NOW MY SON ! NOW IT'S YOUR TURN TO FEEL MY PAIN, DE NINO !" Sylvester's anger got him up from the table and shouted, "YOUR SON WAS AFTER MY DAUGHTERS FOR MONEY, AND NOW YOU WANT TO KILL ME FOR YOUR SON'S SCREW-UPS?" Monica, Renee, and Feng were worried and didn't know what to do out of being shocked. Monica began to beg Stephanie, saying, "Please don't, miss !" Feng then got up slowly. Stephanie saw and yelled, "DON'T !" Monica, Renee, and Feng then saw a man that sat ten feet behind Stephanie get up slowly from his table. The man then reached into his gun holster for his gun, walking with one finger to his lips, signaling to be quiet. Stephanie, watching Feng sit down, then looked at Sylvester, ready to shoot and heard a man's voice from behind yelled, "FREEZE ! … DROP YOUR WEAPON, MISS!" Stephanie then turned around and saw the detective with a gun pointed at her. He repeated again, saying, "Drop your weapon, miss !" Stephanie immediately turned her head back and glanced at Sylvester again in rage, this time yelling, "YOU !" The detective quickly fired one round into her heart and she fell backwards dead immediately. The detective then saw she was dead and looked around, seeing curious faces stare at him. The people were surprised and got up from their seats. The detective then glanced at the gun within a foot from Stephanie's right hand, reaching for his badge from the back pocket. The detective said, "Don't worry, everyone; I'm an officer." The detective then showed his badge, looking at the waiters, surprised near the entrances, and asked, "Where is the manager in this place?"

The detective stood near Stephanie's body, using his cell phone to give a report. After seeing the blood wouldn't stop, he again yelled, "MANAGER, WHERE IS THE MANAGER !" The people around the De Ninos were trying to figure who they were; some had the wrong thoughts based on what they had just witnessed. The manager then ran over from his office to Sylvester, making sure he and his family were ok. The manager passed the cop, saying, "I apologize ! Listen, for as long as I live, you eat for free, sir ! Is everyone ok?" Sylvester, being stunned on the situation, zoned out for a bit. Feng looked at the manager and, out of frustration, yelled, "DID YOU NOT SEE THE COP STANDING OVER THE DEAD BODY?" Sylvester's daughters got up and hugged him with tears. Feng stood close to Sylvester, watching the manager go over to the detective. The customers were all leaving around this time, but one elderly couple stayed. The couple then came over worried for the family. The wife glanced at the girls, saying, "Dear lord ! Are you all in some kind of danger?" Renee, with tears, answered, "No ma'am." The lady then hugged Monica and Renee; her husband was making sure Sylvester was alright. The couple then shortly left.

Twelve minutes later, the police arrived and spoke with the detective that defended the De Nino family standing over the body inside. The detective's name was Ronald and he was tall and lean with short, curly hair. Ronald encouraged Sylvester to stay and go over why the situation had happened. A tall, blonde news reporter named Molly had just shown up with her crew standing outside the restaurant, being blocked by a cop. Within ten minutes, the ambulance arrived and Ronald went outside to speak with them. Sylvester then glanced at the window and saw the police all over. He then told his daughters they were leaving right now in a demanding, loud voice. Feng said, "You don't wanna be on the news I see !" Ronald then came inside the restaurant. He watched Monica and Renee hold their purses ready to leave. Ronald asked, "Do you all wanna tell your version on what had happened here?" Sylvester ignored Ronald and gazed at a waiter near him cleaning a table. Sylvester asked, "Where is the manager?" The manager heard and ran over to Sylvester from the kitchen, asking, "What do you need?"

Sylvester said, "I need a way outta here ! I don't want to talk with no news reporter." The manager understood and said, "Follow me to the back !" Sylvester then looked at Ronald watching them leave and said, "She is dead; you don't need me." Sylvester, Feng, and his two daughters followed the manager and headed to the back door of the restaurant. When they showed up to the back door, the manager then opened the door and they entered into an alley. The manager said, "Mr. De Nino, is there anything else I can do for you?" Sylvester looked around and answered, "There is. Could you send someone to bring my black sports car and a White SUV to this area?" The manager nodding yes, received the keys from Sylvester and Feng said, "Right away, sir !" Feng looked at the manager going inside replied, "We parked to the left !" The manager understood, then called for two employees and gave them orders with the keys. Within ten minutes, the De Ninos and Feng drove to Sylvester's house.

Ronald was talking with two officers at the time and saw the manager come back and give orders in the kitchen. Ronald thought to question the manager, then Molly the news reporter came inside asking the waiters about the De Nino family but got no answers. Molly saw no customers around but cops and the body, which surprised her. Molly then asked, "Has anyone seen these people? I'm the news reporter and I've been waiting for a good ten minutes." Ronald replied, "You can talk to me, miss. I witnessed everything. Let me know when you're ready." The cop that blocked Molly had seen her again, came inside and said, "Miss, you can't be in here. Let's go !" Molly, being curious with her arms crossed, asked, "The officers outside told me very little. Who are you? Where did they go?" The officer, feeling ignored, frowned and said, "Did you hear me? Let's go !" Ronald answered, "I'm Detective Ronald. They left already, miss." Molly looked around and said, "Alright, come with me. My name is Molly by the way." The officer then watched Ronald and Molly pass him, headed outside for the live recording. Molly and Ronald took notice that the situation had caused some traffic watching the camera crew get set up at the entrance.

Vin, at the time, was in the area driving into traffic from work. The traffic had moved and Vin was about to pass the restaurant. Vin saw a cop standing eight feet away, a great crowd. Vin then slowed down and rolled down the window at the passenger side, yelling,"HEY, WHY SO MUCH TRAFFIC?" The officer heard Vin and answered, "Some crazy lady was about to shoot a man or rather a family." Vin frowned at the remark, then asked, "What family?" The officer glanced at the news reporter, then Vin replied, "Some family called De Nino, crazy right?" Vin immediately parked and left the car, hearing a horn from a truck behind him. Vin then saw the body bag around an officer near the ambulance so he ran over to know who it was. The officer saw and stopped Vin, asking, "Who are you?" Vin then gave his name and wanted to know who she was. The officer answered, "Stephanie Lagaipa, do you know her?" The officer then saw her face not closed in the body bag, going inside the ambulance, yelled, "ZIP THE BAG, MAN !" One of the paramedics began to zip up the body bag. Vin saw and was clueless. Vin then began to panic, asking, "What happened? Who did what?" The officer with a serious look again asked, "Do you know her?" Vin denied knowing her, then walked back to his car parked causing traffic. The man in the truck behind him got out and asked, "Is this your car, man? I gotta go to work, bud !" The man then went back inside the truck, frustrated and watching Vin.

Vin ignored the man, leaving heartbroken hearing the cars blow their horns. Vin then drove for a good few minutes and saw a shopping plaza. He immediately drove in and parked. Vin, in rage, said, "Sylvester, if you killed her then I" …. Vin, being angry, then closed his eyes with tears balling his fists. Vin then began to reflect on when he had asked Stephanie to marry him on Thanksgiving at her parents Stephanie, being surprised in the living room in front of her father, said yes. Vin immediately started crying over the loss of Stephanie and their last conversation. Within a few minutes, Vin turned the radio on to hear the news.

Ronald with Molly around that time were ready to give the news, with the camera crew waiting. There stood an officer close to the entry door that stopped Ronald and said, "You're a detective; let me handle this. You told me everything already." Ronald agreed then stood away from the camera to the left side. The camera man then gave the countdown. Molly asked, "What's your name?" The officer gazed into the camera and answered, "Officer Malone." Molly then held the microphone to her lips, focused with a smile, saying, "We are live on Channel one. We have here an officer that can give us information on what took place earlier. What could had been the murder of Sylvester De Nino and his family in downtown New Haven at this Italian restaurant on Bail Street. It was said that the women with a gun was identified as Stephanie Lagaipa ! Officer Malone, can you tell us what brought this on?" Malone replied, "We believe it was out of revenge. Nobody got hurt, which was a miracle in itself. We have many witnesses that saw every-thing, again a miracle."

Meanwhile, watching the news was an officer named Chance. Chance was smart, tall, and dedicated to the law. Chance was seated in the bedroom of his home, dressed casually and waiting for his girlfriend in the bathroom getting ready for dinner. Chance then got upset that the situation had happened at the restaurant they chose. Chance then yelled, "RACHEL ! …. RACHEL !" Rachel then came out in a blue summer dress to know what he wanted, holding a brush. Rachel was short, lean, and caring. Rachel then watched the officer, telling what had happened earlier and that they were close until things got solved. Rachel frowned and went back into the bathroom, saying, "That's just great, you know. I really like that restaurant !" Chance said, "I do too. What about that famous restaurant in Hamden, bae?"

Rachel, upset, started to brush her long, dark hair, looking into the mirror. She then heard the name Feng being mentioned and dropped the brush to the floor. Chance heard the brush drop. He then ran into the bathroom and saw Rachel immediately break down and cry. Chance, not knowing, asked, "What's wrong?" Chance then hugged her, watching tears stream down her cheeks. She gazed at Chance, reflecting on the past with her son. Rachel said, "Take me home !" Chance, not understanding why, replied, "I don't understand? Was it something I said or done? Talk to me ! I wanna know !"

Rachel shook her head no and walked away. Chance then reached for her shoulder and turned her to face him. Rachel then removed his hand and said, "I'm not ready to talk about it !" Rachel then grabbed her purse, leaving the bathroom, and said, "I'll take a cab." Rachel then walked to the living room, being followed by Chance, and stood at the front door, not answering him and calling a cab. Chance, frustrated, continued to talk to her but she wouldn't answer him. He gazed at her, still shedding tears. Rachel in conversation with the cab driver said, "Yes, it's 49 Gardens Road. Yes, please don't pass this address." Rachel then hung up and saw the cab arrived and rushed out of the house, feeling worried and shameful. The cab driver looked back at Rachel coming inside. She then reached into her purse for tissues. The cab driver, looking at her dress, said, "Nice dress, where to, miss?" Rachel then closed the door in thought of Feng wiping her tears and answered, "Far away !" Chance then watched the cab leave through the living room window with the thought of not letting Rachel go.

In that same hour at Sylvester's house, Monica, Feng, and Renee were trying to calm Sylvester down in the living room. Sylvester started to cough a couple times, putting his right hand to his chest. Renee took notice and asked, "Dad, are you alright? Do you need water?" Sylvester looked at her, nodding yes. Renee then rushed into the kitchen to get him a glass of water. Renee reached up into the cabinet near the sink, hearing her father still yelling in worry for the family. Renee began to frown and yelled, "DAD, WILL YOU STOP ALREADY ! …. PLEASE !"

Monica stood in front of her father, saying, "Dad, it's over. Carmen is doing time and his mother is dead. It's over so calm down." Feng stood near the TV, agreeing with Monica and watching Sylvester begin to pace back and forth. Monica stared at Sylvester and said, "We all were at the table with you. I feel good that the cop was there, Pop !" Sylvester then stopped pacing and stared at Monica. Renee then came back and handed him the glass of water. Sylvester held the glass, feeling undermined and stressed out, shouting,

"THE GUN WAS AIMED AT ME, MONICA! …. I DIDN'T WANT THIS FOR THE FAMILY !" Renee, now watching her father drink the water down, comfort him by rubbing his arm said, "Calm down, Pop." Monica, agreeing with her arms crossed, worried about her father's temper. Monica said again, "Dad, it's over. Talk about generational curses, right? …. We don't wanna see you stressed out like this." Sylvester then handed Renee the glass back and began to cool down with a smile, saying, "I'm alright." Feng looked at him and asked, "You good?" Sylvester, being sarcastic, answered, "What did I just say ! …. I'm good, Feng!" Monica and Renee then hugged their father. Sylvester then immediately went back into seeing the gun pointed at him around the table. The girls took notice after they hugged him that he did not look well. Sylvester immediately fell unconscious backwards to the floor.

Feng, Monica, and Renee rushed to Sylvester at once. Feng held and shook Sylvester up, but got no response yelled, "CALL AN AMBULANCE NOW !" Renee had drop the glass, panicking, then reached for her phone at the couch and began to call. Monica sat right by her father, teary-eyed. Monica, not knowing what to do next, began to panic and yelled, "YOU CAN'T DIE ON US, POP ! …. FENG, LET ME HOLD HIM ! …. DON'T DIE PLEASE, DAD !" Feng then moved and let Monica hold him and started to cry. She glanced at Renee and asked, "Renee ! How soon?" Renee, frowning with tears, yelled back, "I DON'T KNOW !" Monica began rocking their father back and forth, hearing Renee mention the address and heart attack. Monica looked up and yelled, "JESUS, PLEASE SAVE MY FATHER !" Renee began to yell on the phone, saying, "HURRY UP! …. OH MY GOD !" Feng stood with Renee in comfort.

Renee gazed at her father, then Monica asked, "Monica, is he breathing? Monica?" Monica, not answering, began to loudly cry. Feng then checked his breathing and answered no. Feng then yelled, "HOW FAR IS THE HOSPITAL FROM HERE?" Renee then got unpleasant and loud on the phone, saying, "I just gave you the address. It's fifty-five Bloom Street. Please hurry !" Renee then looked at Feng and asked again, "Is he breathing now?" Feng shook his head no again, watching Monica rest her head against Sylvester's head, still crying. After Renee finished the phone call, she, not knowing what to do, called Bird. Feng glanced and wondered who she was calling next, asked, "Renee? Who are you calling?" Renee looked away and sat down next to Monica. Feng watch and stood around them.

Bird with Linda at the time were in a crowded restaurant at a table, celebrating their twenty-third year anniversary. They were dressed for the occasion and had only been there for five minutes. The waiter then came over and said, "Hi, I am Tommy. I will be your waiter. Are you two ready to order?" Bird then got a phone call from Renee. He then reached for his phone near the napkins. Bird then saw and thought it was odd said, "I gotta get this. I will be back." Linda watched him go outside to answer. She gazed at the waiter and replied, "Give us a minute." Bird then stood at the entrance and answered, "Hello? Renee, you called?" Renee, in a crying voice, said, "I think my father is dead …. I mean dying !" Bird, not understanding, answered, "What do you mean dying? What happened?" Renee replied, "Heart attack. Heart … Oh my God !" Bird worried then asked,"Where are you all now?" Renee answered, "His house. The ambulance is coming ! I did … I did not know who else to call !" Bird nodded and said, "I'll be right there." Bird then hung up and hurried back to their table. He gazed at Linda and said, "Listen, I … I mean we gotta go, hun!" Linda then got up and loudly asked, "WHY? …. IT'S OUR ANNIVERSARY; AND I DON'T WANNA LEAVE ! …. WHATEVER IT IS ISN'T THAT IMPORTANT, RIGHT?" The people in the restaurant then stopped talking and watched them. Bird took notice and answered, "Sylvester had a heart attack. I'm his children's godfather, you know." Linda then reached for her purse with an attitude. She shook her head out of disgust and said,"I feel you're too dedicated to that family. I mean Marie is dead anyway !" Bird, with a no-nonsense look, got in her face and then loudly said, TOO DEDICATED ? …. THEY NEVER CALL ME ! …. SYLVESTER JUST HAD A HEART ATTACK, AND HOW COULD YOU SAY THAT ABOUT MARIE ! …. HOW COULD YOU !" Linda felt wrong and seen their waiter come over to them. She then walked out of the restaurant upset. The waiter watched her leave and glanced at Bird, asking, "Is everything alright, sir?" Bird took a breather and shook his head no at the remark. He then left hearing the people gossip about their argument.

This story is to be continued. I thank the readers and hope you have enjoyed this story. Please look for the next book coming soon. God bless.

Printed in the USA
CPSIA information can be obtained
at www.ICGtesting.com
JSHW010434241023
50718JS00013B/132